OUR FIRST LEADER

A WELSH FABLE

Jan Morris

First Impression—2000

ISBN 1 85902 852 7

This book is published with the support of the
Arts Council of Wales.

Printed in Wales at
Gomer Press, Llandysul, Ceredigion

CONTENTS

FABULIST'S FOREWORD

Wales is a land of fables. Some of them are fairy fantasies, some are horror stories and some surreal works of art, but a few turn out to develop their own truths. They are self-fulfilling, so to speak.

This one concerns the first President of the Welsh Republic, and it takes its name in happy irony from the title posthumously given to Prince Llywelyn ap Gruffydd, who was killed by the English in 1282. The Welsh sadly called him *Ein Llyw Olaf*, Our Last Leader, because when he died Wales lost its independence to the English under King Edward I.

As everyone now knows, another Llywelyn reversed the process, established the sovereign independence of Wales after so many centuries, and is honoured today as the founder of his nation. It might never have happened – certainly not so abruptly – if the then United Kingdom had not been occupied by the Germans in the second world war, and it is already becoming the stuff of legend. *Our First Leader* tells the tale in its truest, simplest form: for who can doubt that as the centuries pass all manner of epic accretion will change the nature of it, and present to posterity a First Leader of more heroic persona?

PROPOSAL

1 *'See to it Schinkel'*

'See to it Schinkel, would you,' said Gauleiter von Harden to his senior adjutant, 'that when the invitations go out for next week's guest night, they include one for a Dr Parry-Morris, at Jesus College. The first name is probably David, or Samuel, or Moses, or Aaron, or Leviticus. He is a Welshman, and we have a use for him.'

'Should we seat him anywhere special? Is there is a Frau Parry-Morris?'

'Oh next to me, Schinkel, next to me. We will disregard protocol. There is no wife, I believe.'

2 *Dr Parry-Morris is not surprised*

Parry-Morris was not as surprised to be invited as he should have been. Heads of colleges did sometimes dine at the Gauleiter's table, together with distinguished guests from all over Britain, but it was rare for a mere college lecturer to be asked. He was not, however, a modest man. He considered himself well-known in Oxford, as a particular authority on Celtic praise poetry, and he was certainly one of the most public of Welsh nationalists, who had continued to proclaim the patriotic cause of Wales even under the

9

German occupation of Britain – in magazine articles rich in historical allusion, in testy letters to editors, in occasional radio and television interviews. He thought of himself as the spokesman of his country. His first name had in fact once been Samuel, but he had changed it to Llywelyn in tribute to Llywelyn ap Gruffydd, the final hero of independent Wales – changed it partly in tribute, anyway, but partly in the conviction that he himself was called by destiny to the service of his nation.

So as he walked over to Christ Church he was not in the least nervous. Small though he was physically, in his own eyes he towered. He considered himself, as he always did, a natural ambassador, confidently expecting – as it turned out, correctly – to be seated at his host's right hand. He had sometimes had occasion to visit Christ Church since, at the Führer's express command, it had been made the headquarters of the Protectorate Government; but he had not been inside its great Tudor dining hall since the surrender, and he was curious to see what a Nazi-style Oxford guest night was like. Besides, in a half-starved and exhausted Britain, a good German dinner would be welcome.

3 *Within unfortunately inevitable parameters*

'You will find the college very much the same as always,' the Gauleiter assured him as they walked up the rib-vaulted staircase. 'Herr Hitler has been insistent that we honour English tradition as far as possible, and especially the blue-blooded tradition so paramount here at Christ Church. There have been changes of course, but I hope you will find them sympathetic enough, within the unfortunately inevitable parameters of circumstance.' Certainly at first sight all seemed reassuring. The long rows of portraits still hung on the walls. The old oak tables were still well-polished. The silver shone. The lower tables, where the undergraduates used to eat, were occupied by the hundreds of young officers and bureaucrats of the headquarters, together with their wives. At high table Parry-Morris recognized a few familiar faces – two or three college heads with their wives, Lord Brackenthorpe, Minister for Minorities in the British Associate Government, down from London for the night – together with a plethora of senior military officers, party functionaries and handsome blonde ladies, some with braids. It was true that the great Holbein painting of Henry VIII, at the head of the room, had been replaced by a full-length picture of Adolf Hitler (rumoured in Oxford to be a self-portrait), and that the shambling college servants of the old days had given way to smart young soldiers. But the smell was still the old smell, of age and wood and wine and food, and the Gauleiter himself, banging the table for attention with his hammer of chastened silver, briskly said the brief old grace – *Benedictus, benedicat.*

4 *Courteous enough conversation*

'You see,' he said, tucking his napkin in his collar, 'all much the same – even most of the same alumni portraits, which you must admit is evidence of enlightened attitudes. There's Gladstone, you see! There's Lewis Carroll! Even the decadent Auden!'

'It is a pity nevertheless,' said Parry-Morris, 'that King Henry VIII no longer presides over our feast. He was, as you know, a Welsh-speaking Welshman. As to the three personalities you have plucked from these serried ranks of the famous, you have chosen, Herr Gauleiter, delicately. Gladstone's home at Hawarden in Flintshire was admittedly rather near the English border, but he was an earnest advocate of self-rule for Wales. Lewis Carroll, as I'm sure you know, immortalized Llandudno through the medium of *Alice in Wonderland*. And I have reason to believe that the name 'Auden' (although in personal matters, I agree, the poet did not invariably do it honour) is hardly more than a crude corruption of the old Welsh word *odlwr*, meaning a rhymester or bard, a most suitable if inadvertent nomenclature. Have you learnt a few words of Welsh yourself during your stay in these islands?'

'Unfortunately not. I came here, as you know, directly from the *General gouvernment* in Krakow, and my duties are very pressing: but I have every intention of devoting some time to the language during my next period of leave.'

He was lying of course, the Welsh language standing exceedingly low in his list of intellectual priorities: but so the conversation proceeded, courteously enough, as they ate their roast veal and drank their burgundy ('fortunately we have access to supplies even in these difficult times') until they adjourned to the former senior common-room and the Gauleiter, his glass of port in his hand, invited Parry-Jones to withdraw with him into a quiet corner of the room. 'Please see we're not disturbed, Schinkel, there's a good fellow.'

5 The Führer's particular interest

'As you may know,' von Harden began in a decidedly confidential tone of voice, 'the Führer takes a particular interest in your people, and has instructed me to make them an especial concern of mine. He has never forgotten his meetings with your charismatic Lloyd George. We realize of course that you Welsh are not an Aryan race in the generally accepted sense, but you are a nation that has preserved its ethnic purity, and its *volk*-consciousness, through many centuries of English oppression and interference. We recognize and respect such fortitude. It is a quality that we pride in ourselves, too.'

'Most certainly, Herr Gauleiter,' interjected Parry-Morris, 'your worst enemies cannot deny you that. Your continuing battle against the godless Soviets is testimony to an inherited resolution of principle and conviction that I believe I may say the old chapel culture of the Welsh, and particularly of the rural Welsh amongst whom our language and traditions have been most dauntlessly maintained, has itself demonstrated down the long centuries of our national servitude.'

'Well, Morris-Jones,' laughed the Gauleiter, 'anyone would know you were a Welshman! I wonder what that wonderfully musical sentence would sound like in Welsh?'

'Everything is more beautiful in the language of God.'

'Quite so,' said the Gauleiter, not knowing what else to say, and proceeded with his theme. 'We well understand too how insidious have been the inroads of Englishness upon your ancient ways – the constant flow of English immigrants over your borders, the incessant inroads of English radio, television, the Press, all that kind of thing, tempered though their worst vulgarities have been, I think it fair to say, since our Protectorate was established.'

'Undeniably, and we thank you for it – although I must make clear to you that your own ideology is most distasteful to me – I must be frank with you about that – I am not, and never shall be, a Fascist – let me make that quite clear.'

'Of course, of course, calm yourself dear man. We do not expect even some of our best friends to agree with us. But I hope you will be in agreement with a new policy towards Wales, which has been promulgated in Germania and which I have been empowered to implement. We are calling it the Welsh Dimension, and it is this. The Führer has been so impressed by your record of national intransigence that he wishes to help you achieve what I know you yourself yearn for, Parry-Morris: namely complete national independence, cultural, ethnic and political. He wishes to free and separate you once and for all from England, and enable you to live by your own values in your own dear Homeland. Cimry will be a nation once again, confident and unsullied.'

'Cymru.'

'I beg your pardon?'

'Cymru – the name of our country is pronounced as though it were to be spelt Cumry in the English tongue. The origins of the word are debatable, but it is generally agreed to bear some connotation of 'fellowship' – 'comradeship' if you like, although the con-tonality is purely fortuitous.'

'Oh forgive me, Herr Doctor – but never hesitate to correct me on such matters. I wish only to be correct towards the Welsh nation, as the Führer particularly wishes. Come now, Dr Parry-Morris, will you drink with me, as allies in this if in nothing else, to a new future for your beloved country – *Cymru*? (You see! We do try!)'

6 *Taking a speculative sip*

The arrangements for the new Welsh future were already, it turned out, far advanced. The first thing had been to decide who the Welsh were. 'In this we have relied upon the native patriotism of your people. You may remember that in the Protectorate census which we conducted last year the populace was invited to register its race. I am quite sure that you yourself proudly entered 'Welsh,' and knowing the nature of your compatriots we can be sure that virtually every Welsh person did the same, both within Wales itself and outside its borders. You will not be offended when I say that very few Englishmen or Scots would have registered themselves as being Welsh, so for a start we have decided that the Welsh nation shall consist

15

entirely of those who have declared themselves to be Welsh.'

'*Da iawn*,' said Parry-Morris. 'Excellent.'

Next there was the matter of Homeland territory. It would be impractical, the Gauleiter said, simply to make the whole of Wales a separate entity from the start. The industrialized south of the country, and the north-east, was so heavily Anglicized that for the moment at least it would be excluded, and the whole of the coastline was a military zone. A new border would, in effect, create a Wales that was compact, rural, uncrowded and inhabited overwhelmingly still by Welsh people, most of them Welsh-speaking. It would include three small market towns – Machynlleth, Dolgellau and Llanidloes (although the Gauleiter had some difficulty in pronouncing them) – besides the mountainous northern area called Eryri. Into this confined but beautiful region, to be dubbed New Wales – '*Cymru Newydd*!' cried Parry-Morris – all those who had registered themselves as Welsh would be encouraged to move, and from it all English people would be induced to emigrate.

'*Bendigedig*,' said Parry-Morris, 'a blessed solution for which we have long been working.'

It might perhaps be argued, continued the Gauleiter, that the increased population of these parts would not be economically viable: but so great was the demand for supplies of all sorts on the continuing Siberian front – where victory was inevitable of course in the long run, but would probably take many more years to achieve – that the High Command had suggested building a number of munitions factories in Welsh

16

Wales, providing work for all and giving the people a common sense of unity and purpose.

'I am myself a pacifist, of course,' said Parry-Morris, 'but I cannot deny the validity and practicality of the proposal.'

'So we have it,' said the Gauleiter. 'We have identified the people. We have delimited the territory. We have arranged the economic basis of nationhood. We are assured of the loyalty and enthusiasm of the citizenry. All that remains, Dr Parry-Morris, but it is a very big, a very important factor in our equation – all that we need is the leadership.'

Parry-Morris took another speculative sip of his port (he used to be something of a connoisseur of ports), and shifted slightly in his arm-chair.

'You will have guessed by now why I have invited you here this evening. Is there anyone else with the conviction, the ability, the fire, may I say the love to undertake this task? To lead a great people back into their ancient pride and sovereignty? As the Protecting Power we can do so much, but only so much. We can set up what our economists call the infra-structure, arrange the logistics, provide the wherewithal and the know-how. But we cannot provide the inspiration – the Welshness. We cannot provide a leader for the Welsh.

'Will you be that leader, Dr Parry-Morris? Will you give our grand enterprise the stamp of truth?'

7 *'A nation must be guided'*

As he saw the Welshman to the door, and looked out
with him into the night across the quadrangle, where
the helmeted sentries paced, the Gauleiter took Parry-
Morris's elbow and pressed it warmly. 'I am so glad
you have agreed,' he said. 'May the stars be rising upon
a new and glorious Wales! But there is one matter I
ought perhaps to have mentioned – or perhaps I do not
need to. We cannot achieve our purpose without an
element of, how shall I phrase it, compulsion. You do
realize that?'

'Alas, it was always so. A nation must be guided
even towards the greatest ends. That is an evil we must
bear. We are a people used to afflictions. We shall rise
above it, for the sake of our nation. Good night to you,
Herr Gauleiter, and *Cymru am byth*!'

Von Harden, not being quite sure what this gnomic
valediction meant, returned a guarded *Heil Hitler*, and
the sentries, passing at that moment by the common-
room door, respectfully saluted. They were kilted
soldiers of the Bonnie Prince Charlie SS Division.

8 *Living in a naughty world*

'Well, sir,' said Schinkel. 'How was the Welsh
wizard? Did he enchant you?'

'A bit of a fool, Schinkel, but a not unbeguiling fool.
Was his first name Biblical, by the way?'

'Samuel on his birth record, something very Welsh
on his papers.'

'Aha. But they are a beguiling people, I think. In a way I rather regret their racial ambivalences. As it is . . . Ah well, good night Schinkel. We live in a naughty world.'

'Good night, sir,' said the adjutant. 'I'm glad it all went well. I thought the veal was excellent, didn't you? And that Lord Brackenthorpe is a real charmer.'

INVITATION

1 *An Inviter is appointed*

For some months Parry-Morris was left to pursue his own work (a pamphlet about the effect of metrical psalmody upon northern Welsh folk-narratives, and a contribution to the new Oxford Companion to Celtic Dialectic – besides, of course, his usual tutorial and lectoral duties). The Germans proceeded with the Welsh Dimension, but so restricted were communications within occupied Britain, so rigidly censored was the Press, that by and large the general public knew nothing of it, and Parry-Morris himself was kept informed only by occasional telephone calls from the Gauleiter. 'Your day is coming, Parry-Morris,' von Harden assured him once. '*Der Tag*, what? Rest assured that all is in hand, and that when the moment approaches for you to join your people in your ancestral homeland, we shall let you know in good time. "Be Prepared." Isn't that what the scout boys say? In the meantime I have placed in charge of the Dimension one of the very best of my adjutants, Heinrich Schinkel – perhaps you met him at dinner that evening? A delightful officer. I know you will like him. We have given him the temporary official title of *Reich-Einlandinger* – the Reich-Inviter, would you say?'

2 *What they meant by popular readjustments*

What was happening was this. The Reich-Kontrolle organization was erecting a frontier line around the borders of Cymru Newydd. It was made partly of concrete walling, partly of barbed wire rolls, and it had frontier posts at three entry points, two for road traffic, one for a railway line. They were manned only by elderly Wermacht reservists. ('These are a sensitive people we are dealing with, Schinkel,' as the Gauleiter said, 'we must not upset their susceptibilities by confusing the Dimension with other such operations in the East – none of your glorious SS men, now, for the moment at least'). At the same time compulsory movement orders were delivered to all those many residents of Wales who had declared themselves English in the recent census: families were instructed to report at Machynlleth, more or less the central town of Wales, for the special trains which would take them to relocation areas in England. This was called popular readjustment, and since it was accompanied by all manner of obligatory movements throughout Britain – the shifting of labour here and there, posting to work forces in eastern Europe, building detachments transfer, social service conscription, medical volunteer levies, ethnic distributions according to the Protectorate Master-Plan – in such a climate of uncertainty, designed not only to help the Reich's war effort, but also to keep the indigenes in a condition of bewildered apprehension, the movement of a few hundred thousand people out of Wales went generally unnoticed.

The remaining Welsh within Wales were moved into the thousand-odd square miles of Cymru Newydd. They were promised full-time jobs within months, and most of them willingly went. Those from the derelict industrial areas hoped for better living conditions, those from rural parts were glad to leave a countryside denied virtually all means of transport or communication. In the settlement areas new factories began to appear, simple but workmanlike, and Welsh managers from the industrial areas beyond the Dimension prepared them for production under the guidance of experts from Krupp and Siemen. Rows of accommodation huts went up too, to await the arrival of the Welsh from the diaspora.

3 *Protectorate Law 2607*

'How are you wording the Invitation, Schinkel? Not in any harsh or hectoring way? Remember we are inviting them to their fulfilment.'

'I'll show you, sir. I have proofs here. At the moment they are only in German and English, but they are being translated into Welsh too.'

'By Parry-Morris?'

'Who else? Only the wordiest, for the Welsh Dimension.'

'Now, now, Schinkel, show some respect.'

This is the Invitation instruction that von Harden read:

Welsh Men, Women and Children!

Under the terms of the Welsh Dimension, ordered by our beloved Führer, each one of you is entitled to a free return, with transport provided by the Protectorate Government, to the dear Land of your Fathers, where new homes and work for all will be awaiting you. There you will be enabled to live according to the true traditions of your ancestors, liberated at last from English oppression, reunited with your compatriots and honouring a culture which has survived all setbacks during the 1,000 years since your noble nation was denied its independence. You are therefore invited to proceed on [date blank], being sure to take all your papers with you, together with no more possessions than you can personally carry, to [name blank] railway station for speedy repatriation.

Failure to comply with this invitation is punishable by Protectorate Law 2607

> *'Aros mae'r mynyddau mawr*
> *Rhuo trostynt mae y gwynt*
> *Clywir eto gyda'r wawr*
> *Gân bugeiliaid megis cynt . . .'*

HEIL HITLER! – HAIL HITLER! – HENFFYCH HITLER!

(signed) Heinrich Schinkler, Reich-Inviter

'What is Law 2607?' asked the Gauleiter.

'It is what you might call an *ad hoc* law, sir.'

'Aha. I like the *Heil Hitler* bit, very good. But what's this poetical gibberish?'

'That was a Parry-Morris addition. He said it would be inspiring. It's all about mountains and shepherds.'

'He wrote it?'

'I gather not. He said it was by a bard. We shall print it in green, which is the national colour. What a lot one does learn, in the course of one's duty to the Reich.'

4 *Parry-Morris is reassuring*

Dr Parry-Morris had been quite pleased with the wording of the Invitation, except for the line about Law 2607 ('a mere formality, I assure you,' Schinkel said, 'we are obliged to say such things. Actually there is no Law 2607') He was touched by the inclusion of *Aros mae*, and the idea of printing it in green was his own. He readily admitted to his part in it when one morning his pupil Emrys Owen, from Kingston-upon-Thames, confided that he and all the members of his family had received copies through the mail.

'Ah,' he exclaimed, 'so it is happening! You fortunate people, to be the first generation of the Return. The prophecies are coming true! You remember that poem of Llywarch Hen which we discussed a week or two ago? Surely that foreshadowed what is coming to pass today. I cannot deny that the agency of our fulfilment is hardly what I could wish it to be – as you know, young Emrys, I have never for a moment been sympathetic towards any kind of totalitarian regime, be it Norman or Nazi: but God often moves in mysterious ways, as was written by one of the best non-Welsh hymn-writers, who nevertheless may be said to have exerted some influence upon *Pantycelyn* and even Ann Griffiths. 'He plants his footsteps in the sea, and rides upon the storm'

– remember that, Emrys, and be grateful that you and your dear family will be among the first to see Cymru reborn, Cymru itself again!'

'But what about this Law 2607?' said Emrys. 'We none of us like the sound of that.'

'Don't let it alarm you. I know the officer in charge of the Welsh Dimension, a very decent sort of man, genuinely interested in matters Welsh, particularly Welsh poesy, and he has assured me that it is mentioned purely as a matter of bureaucratic necessity. Anyway, my dear boy, who would not leap at the chance of witnessing the very start of a new Cymru? Are you not yourself eager to stand as a free citizen on your own beloved soil?'

'I'm not entirely sure,' said Emrys Owen. 'I've never been there.'

5 The blossoming of Parry-Morris

Once the general details of the Welsh Dimension were published in the official Press, Parry-Morris was much in demand to explain them. It was announced that when the framework of the new Cymru were established, he would be returning to his homeland to take up the responsibilities of Y Llyw, The Leader – not, as he was anxious to tell everybody, a mere translation of the German title, but the revival of one of the most ancient of Welsh honorifics. 'Ein Llyw Olaf, Our Last Leader – that is what my people have always called Llywelyn ap Gruffydd, the last of our independent Cymric princes.'

Within his college, traditionally the Welsh college of Oxford University, he had to fight off suggestions that he was no more than a collaborator with the enemy. He did it with aplomb. Using the power of the Germans to re-establish the nationhood of Wales was no more despicable, he said, than striking up an alliance with the Communists to fight off the Fascists. 'Mr Churchill had no qualms, as he himself said, in supping with the devil in a righteous purpose: similarly I do not fear the judgement of Our Creator in accepting the help of a wicked Power for the fulfilment of a noble, historic and socially justifiable end. We have an old saying in our language – better the rusty saw than the knife without a blade. That, gentlemen, is the justification of my actions.' His colleagues were not entirely convinced – 'trust the bloody Jerries to get hold of that old clown,' was the comment of one of the younger dons – but the whole nature of the Welsh Dimension had been left so deliberately vague, and the emotions and perceptions of all Britain had been so blunted by the tragedy of defeat, that on the whole he was given the benefit of the doubt.

In a wider arena, anyway, he was accorded more respect. The Germans saw to that. No British radio or television studio was without its official co-director, no newspaper lacked its resident censor; his coming appointment was dutifully if not obsequiously reported. In his many interviews with the media, in TV chat shows and radio phone-ins, Parry-Morris was able to express himself as never before. Marvellous flights of historical fancy illuminated his talk. Curled horsemen of Welsh antiquity rode through his explanations, elaborate genealogies illustrated his arguments, names like Sion ap Siencyn ap Huw ap Meredydd resounded over the airwaves in evening discussion programmes.

He did not blush to express his gratitude to the authorities of the Protectorate, for enabling this consummation to be achieved at last. He realized that thanks to the patronage of the Protectorate Propaganda Department, for the first time English people in general were really being made aware of the historical existence of Wales, its rights as a nation, the wrongs it had endured under the centuries of English rule. They even learnt to call it Cymru, and pronounce it properly, too. They even grew to like Parry-Morris. 'You have to hand it to the little fart,' said the young don, 'he's got the gift of the gab.'

6 *'Parry-Morris believes it'*

'You're giving this fellow Parry-Morris a lot of rope, aren't you Gauleiter?' said Lord Brackenthorpe the Minorities Minister one day. 'Are you hoping he'll hang himself?'

'Dear me no, not at all. In the Protectorate Government we have a high opinion of his abilities, and greatly value his contribution to the evolution of the Welsh Dimension.'

'Pull the other one,' said Lord Brackenthorpe.

'Ha, ha! 'Pull the other one'! I do so admire the wealth and variety of the English vernacular. No, but seriously, we are grateful to Parry-Morris. He is performing of course within parameters that we ourselves have decreed, and is doing a good job, I feel, in publicizing our genuine respect for the idea of Welsh nationhood, and our intention to restore full Welsh independence in a true national home. Now he is usefully disseminating our policies to the general public; when he takes up his duties as Y Llyw – you are familiar with the phrase? It means The Leader – as I say, when he returns to Cymru himself and assumes his official duties, his presence will be a reassurance to the world of our benevolent intentions.'

'If the world believes that, it will believe anything,' said Lord Brackenthorpe.

'Oh, I don't know,' said the Gauleiter. 'Parry-Morris believes it.'

FAREWELL

1 *The Invitation takes effect*

Gradually, as the weeks passed, the Invitation began to take effect, and from several English railway centres trains full of Welsh people rumbled off into the west. They were comfortable enough passenger trains, and though they were horribly jammed, and the Invitees were able to take only a minimum of baggage, still the faces that crowded the compartment windows were not despondent. Most of them were quite exuberant. Hardly a soul had failed to hear one or another of Parry-Morris's uplifting radio talks, or to see him performing with such persuasive old-school charm on television shows. Life was miserable enough in England anyway: even those who had not thought of themselves as Welsh for years, even for generations, felt some sense of adventure as they chugged away towards their national home. Those who spoke Welsh were kindly encouraging to those who did not – they'd soon pick it up. Those who had previously been to Wales spoke warmly of its beauties to those who had never been nearer than Birmingham. The trains were festooned with Welsh dragon flags, and often people at level crossings heard the sound of grand Welsh choral singing as the coaches clattered by.

OX1

The first of these transports, numbered OX1, had symbolically started from Oxford – symbolically partly because it was the capital of the German Protectorate, the seat of the Gauleiter, and partly because Dr Parry-Morris lived there. Since the depression of the 1930s a large Welsh population had settled around the industrial plants in the suburb of Cowley, too, and there had always been a Welsh presence at the University. The very first Invitation Special, then, set off on March 1st, St David's Day, the national day of Wales, from the station on the Botley road. Of course Dr Parry-Morris went to see it off, wearing in his lapel a large leek, traditionally the national symbol, in preference to the daintier daffodil which was by then more commonly sported. He drove to the station with the Reich-Inviter, sitting in the back of his big black Mercedes with its fluttering swastikas. Armed guards rode in the open car behind, and there was a motor-cycle escort which swarmed dashingly and menacingly around them as they swept into the station yard.

The Invitees were already seated in the train, and a band was playing on the station platform – not a military band, Parry-Morris was pleasantly surprised to discover, but the Cowley Motor Works Brass Band. They played a selection of Old Welsh Airs as the official party walked up and down the train, followed by a gaggle of cameramen and reporters. 'You'd better go first, Parry-Jones,' said the Inviter, 'you're going to be the Leader': and so, as the folk-melodies rang through the station, the diminutive Llyw-Designate in

30

his blue overcoat paced along the platform followed by officials of the Protectorate Government, liaison officers from the Associate Government and representatives of the Oxford City Council. Several acquaintances looked out at Parry-Morris from the windows of the train.

The Invitees were seated according to their eventual destinations – Machynlleth settlers in one coach, Llanidloes in another, Dolgellau in a third. Emrys Owen waved diffidently at the Llyw-Designate from the Llanidloes coach: in the one marked 'Machynlleth,' named as the administrative capital of Cymru Newydd, Parry-Morris was for a moment perturbed to see the severe brooding face of Sir Gwilym Adam-Jones, Master of Jesus College, together with his fierce wife Miriam and their unexpectedly pretty daughter Angharad. It was like the inspection of a guard of honour. The faces of the Invitees looked blankly out, not knowing quite how to respond, and sometimes Parry-Jones paused, to mouth a greeting to some university acquaintance, bow ingratiatingly to ladies, or wiggle his fingers at an infant. The Germans paused behind him, smiling too. When they came to the engine Parry-Morris stopped to exchange a word or two, in the royal manner, with the driver, leaning out of his cab window. 'A Welshman too?' said the Llyw. 'Not bloody likely,' said the driver.

Unabashed, Parry-Morris mounted a small dais, Schinkel at his side, to make a short farewell speech. Few of the Invitees could hear him, but it did not matter: the radio microphones and TV cameras were there.

'Dear friends and fellow-countrymen,' he said. 'At this historic moment in the history of our nation I come to offer you my congratulations, my good wishes, and – yes, my envy! I shall be coming very soon myself to Cymru Newydd, to assume my duties as your Llyw, but how I would like to be able to claim that I was among the first to return to a Wales that was a true nation again – that I had ridden on the train OX1, like those heroic forebears of ours, in the days of Prince Madog, who were the first to brave the Atlantic waves and discover America. They found a new world: you, better still, are off to find a new Wales! Bon voyage dear friends! Au revoir! Good luck to Train OX1 and all who ride in her!'

The engine rumbled. The cameras whirred. The band struck up *Hen Wlad Fy Nhadau*, 'Land of Our Fathers,' the Welsh national anthem, and Parry-Morris wiped a tear from his eye as the train moved off. The last face he saw, staring at him fixedly out of the window, was that of Sir Gwilym Adam-Jones, with Miriam glaring over his shoulder. 'Au revoir, dear Master!' breathed the Llyw-Designate, waving his large white handkerchief.

3 *Saying goodbye to the band*

Before they left the station, they said goodbye to the band. 'Many of them are Welshmen,' Schinkel explained to Parry-Morris, 'and will be going themselves on later trains: in the meantime they have freely given of their time to enliven the departures of Invitees.'

'Yes, that's perfectly true, Dr Parry Morris sir,' said the silver-epauletted bandmaster. 'We've heard a number of your radio broadcasts sir, and we felt quite uplifted by them, felt quite a bit of the old *hwyl* as it were, and so we said to ourselves in committee, we said, why not volunteer our services to the old cause, while we await our own turn to go? I hope that wasn't an impertinence of us, sir.'

'Impertinence, my dear friend! How could a service *dros Gymru*, for Wales, ever be an impertinence! Just as the Welsh princes of old were honoured to be musicked by the great bards and harpers of antiquity – I would instance Iolo Goch singing the praises of the great Owain Glyndŵr – just so, I say, does the company assembled here today receive, with precisely the same humility and gratitude, the beautiful playing of your ensemble.'

'The committee will be very relieved to hear it, sir. We did wonder about the propriety of it, though it is true that in the past we were more than once highly praised by the adjudicators of the National Eisteddfod.'

'Well done, Bandmaster,' Schinkel said.

ARTISTRIES

1 *Far away in Germania*

The Inviter reported to the Gauleiter, in all amusing detail, the events of the morning. The Gauleiter lifted his telephone and reported to the Führer himself, far away in his imperial capital Germania, that OX1 had departed. One might suppose that the ruler of all Europe would hardly be very interested, but it was true that Adolf Hitler had a particular interest in the destiny of the Welsh, and had charged von Harden to keep him informed on every development of the Dimension.

It was many years since the final victory in Europe. Although the German armies were still mired in their apparently interminable war against Soviet Russia, and Soviet hit-and-run bombers occasionally raided German cities, the Reich was now firmly established throughout the continent. Berlin had been transformed into Germania, and the Führer had moved into the awesome new Chancellory which Albert Speer had designed for him. The walls of its operation room were covered with maps, but only a few of them illustrated the course of the fighting in the east, which had subsided into a trench warfare of stalemate. Most of them were concerned with Europe's racial condition, the progress of Nazi Germany's determination to make the Third Reich ethnically pure and logical. By now the master-map of this series was almost all white. Nearly

34

all the most irrational minorities had been eliminated in one way or another, down to the Karaim of Lithuania and the very last of the Wends, while all the Slavs had been re-graded as *untermensch*. Only a small question mark, over in the west of the continent, marked the continuing existence of another untidy and unnecessary minority, the Welsh.

It was years since the Führer had realized his own destiny to be somehow linked with this most obscure of his subjects. He had known since the 1940s, because one of the most trustworthy of his astrologers had told him, that March 1st, in the House of Pisces, would play a fateful part in his life: after the occupation of Britain it came to his ears (actually when Goering appropriated for himself the title Prince of Wales) that March 1 had long been the national festival of the Welsh. He had not given a thought to the existence of the people since the visit of the Welsh political leader David Lloyd George to Berchtesgarden long before the war, a visit which, he now recalled in his old age, had left him with a peculiarly disturbed sensation, not quite sure whether he had duped the Welshman, or the Welshman had duped him. He took to reading books about the Welsh, most of them especially translated for him from English, and in one of them he discovered the disturbing claim, advanced by some Welshmen, that they were in fact the Lost Tribes of Israel. They sometimes looked rather Jewish, the Führer learnt. They shared some of the Jewish characteristics. They gave their children names straight from the Old Testament. They were disputatious, musical, keen on ancient genealogies and often pacifist.

'Mark Wales black on the map,' Hitler had then said
to Heinrich Himmler.

2 *A glint in the corner of a masterpiece*

'*Jawohl*,' said Himmler. 'But *mein Führer*,'
intervened Josef Goebbels, and his slinky voice calmed
the dictator. 'Should we not move carefully?
Expungement shall of course be the eventual fate of the
Welsh, but it would be wise to be subtle of approach.'
The truth was that the German Empire, though
powerful, rich and internally peaceful, was still isolated
in the world. Some Americans in particular, greatly
though they had admired the Nazi stand against
Communism, and welcomed the abolition of the
British Empire, were beginning to suspect that the New
Europe, far from being a kind of European United
States as they had been so skilfully persuaded, was
really no more than another imperialism. Over in
Ottawa the aged Churchill was still agitating for
revenge, broadcasting all the time and constantly down
in Washington toadying to the President, and the King
and Queen of England were still hanging about over
there. It would be decades before the New Order was
finally recognized as permanent. Countless pernicious
influences across the seas, refugees, renegades, Jews,
not to mention the Soviet Communists, were working
for its downfall; the Indians and Chinese were never to
be trusted; even the Japanese sometimes seemed less
than reliable. Above all there was always the
possibility that one day the immense power of

America, gathering around it the resources of all Germany's old enemies, would be hurled against the Reich.

'Nonsense!' said Hitler. 'The Americans are just a pack of decadent carniverous Jew-lovers.'

'Certainly they are,' said silver-tongued Goebbels, 'but it would surely be wise to keep manipulating their opinions. So I have a suggestion to make about the Welsh, Adolf. Before we rid ourselves of them, before healthy labour for the Fatherland wears them out, let us use them to show the world that ours is truly a New Order, more than a mere imposition, but a genuine association of loyal peoples under the auspices of the Third Holy German Reich. The Welsh have long chafed, I am told, beneath the rule of the English: let us give them their sovereign freedom, eh, *mein Führer*, let us make a nation of them, eh, let us send them to a promised land, eh, eh? The world will admire our generous enlightenment, and when it is all over with them – well, it will all be over. Work will make them free, eh *mein Führer*?'

'Dear Goebbels, you are an artist,' said Adolf Hitler. 'I am an artist too. I manipulate history as an artist. My brush-strokes are generally large and lavish, powerful strokes, the paintwork of command, but I recognize too, Goebbels, the artistry of the miniature, the little stipple in the corner, the water-colour touch. We will use these shit as a little detail in our masterpiece. They will be a glint in the corner, the degenerate neo-Biblical scum, before we blot them out.'

And so the Welsh Dimension had been conceived, and so Parry-Morris caught the eye of Miriam Adam-

Jones in the compartment window, and the Cowley
Motors Silver Band played 'Land of my Fathers' on
platform 1.

3 *A particularly exclusive honour*

'The Führer is delighted by the way it all went,' the
Gauleiter told the Inviter. 'You will probably get a
medal out of this.'

'Surely, sir, any medal should rightly be yours.'

'It's good of you to say so, dear boy, but really I
have plenty already. Did you know the Associate
Government is to make me a Knight of the Garter for
the achievement of the Dimension? It is a particularly
exclusive honour, I am told.'

PREPARATION

1 *The dodderer's doubts*

Some members of the Associate Government, still in theory the sovereign authority in the United Kingdom, were not pleased with the development of the Welsh Dimension, and raised the matter with the Reich Adviser at one of their Cabinet meetings in London. 'Does this not,' asked the Prime Minister, 'rather bely the spirit of the Association Pact, which guaranteed the integrity of the British nation-State?' He said it without much conviction, because he knew that the office of Reich Adviser was much more than advisory, and that Hermann Thorssen, formerly a well-known hanging judge, was not there for the exchange of ideas. Sure enough, 'The Dimension, Prime Minister,' said Thorssen, 'is a particular concern of the Führer himself, and I do not think any of us would wish to thwart his desires.'

'No, no, certainly not, of course not, but I just wondered . . .'

'Keep your wondering to yourself, Jack,' said Lord Brackenthorpe his Minorities Minister, 'that's my advice. You know damn well the Welsh have always been a perfect curse to us all. Now you're going to be rid of the lot of them. Thank God for small mercies, what Thorssen?'

'Thank the Führer, Brackenthorpe,' Thorssen piously replied.

'Still,' said the Prime Minister, 'I can't help remembering the happy holidays we used to have at Aberystwyth when I was a child. We went there every year for years and years. People actually talk the Welsh language there, you know Thorssen – they gabble away like anything – quite incomprehensible of course to anyone else. Our old landlady up there was a delightful old soul, I remember, very fond of us children. Very fond of cats too. 'Now, now pussy,' she used to say, 'let the kiddies have their tea first, then you shall have your milk – kiddies first, cats second, because cats don't pay rent.' That's what she used to say, dear old soul, 'cats don't pay rent.' Ah me, how long ago it was – before some of you young chaps were born.'

But everyone knew he was an old dodderer, or the Germans wouldn't have made him Prime Minister.

2 *Unable to accept informal hospitality*

Meanwhile the resettlement of the Welsh Diaspora continued. 'Plenty of time,' the Gauleiter told Schinkel, 'plenty of time. Remember we intend that the eyes of the world shall be upon this little operation, and we will play it the gentlemanly way, the English way.'

'Dear me, sir,' said Schinkel, 'Parry-Morris wouldn't like to hear that!'

'Oh, my word no, I hadn't thought of that. How is he, by the way? We must have him to dinner once more before he goes. We'll get Brackenthorpe down too.

He's always funny about Parry-Morris and the Welsh – I sometimes think, don't you Schinkel, that the English sense of humour is crueller than our own? What is your view?'

'I don't think you have to be very cruel to be funny about Our Last Leader.'

What a shock, when Parry-Morris declined the invitation! Nobody had ever declined an invitation to the Gauleiter's table before, unless you counted the late Dean of Christ Church in the unfortunate months immediately after the surrender. 'Never mind,' von Harden told the Protectorate Council, when the matter cropped up at their weekly meeting. 'Parry-Morris has explained to me in his inimitable way that he feels no longer able to accept hospitality of an informal kind from the Protectorate. He says – listen to this, this will amuse you – he says as the Llyw-Designate of a sovereign nation he would feel it improper to dine with the Reich-Gauleiter except with full diplomatic protocol. Did you ever hear anything like it? He really is priceless. Schinkel, would you set up something more suitable for Our Last Leader, something of more diplomatic propriety? Just half a dozen of us, in the Chapter House perhaps? Make sure the photographers are there – and have them put some flags up will you, swastika and red dragon intertwined, that sort of thing. What fun it all is – don't you think so, gentlemen?'

Oh great fun, Gauleiter, thought the members of the Council, most entertaining.

Parry-Morris did not, of course, think it fun at all. When the new invitation arrived ('Full dress, medals will be worn') he wrote to the Gauleiter to express his appreciation. 'You will understand, Gauleiter, that a nation cannot be restored to sovereignty without the full implementation of the correct protocol. I realize that set against the scale of the New Europe, Cymru is small indeed, but I think I can claim that we make up for our physical smallness with our ancient heritage of pride and poetry. I am gratified, Herr Gauleiter, that you share this view with such delicacy.' Von Harden read out his letter at the next Council meeting, and all the councillors thought it quaint and charming.

3 *People about in the quad*

As the Dimension trains trundled off, month after month, England gradually became *Welsch-frei*, and Parry-Morris began to run out of pupils. Many of his teaching colleagues at Jesus College, too, no longer appeared, and no new Master was appointed to replace Adam-Jones. From time to time postcards arrived from Cymru Newydd, but like all internal mail in the Protectorate they were heavily censored, and generally reported merely that all was going well. Parry-Morris protested strongly to the Reich-Inviter that at least they might be written in Welsh, but Schinkel much regretted that there were insufficient Welsh-speaking censors to permit it. 'All will be different, Llyw, when you yourself return to Cymru and take command.'

The first anniversary of OX1 was named as the day of that return, and of the official establishment of Cymru Newydd – C-Day, the German propagandists called it. By then all the invitees would be re-settled, the last English would long have left Wales and the new factories would be working. In the meantime, since he had so little work to do in college, Parry-Morris set up his own temporary Leader's Office in a couple of rooms overlooking the front quadrangle of Jesus College, with a flag flying from a flagstaff outside its windows. He liked to say that these had been the rooms of Lawrence of Arabia, as an undergaduate in the college before the first world war – 'he was born in Tremadog, you know, in the ancient commote of Eifionydd, and came to Jesus on a Welsh scholarship.'

The Germans indulged him in his fancies, and sometimes took eminent guests along to call on him. The deputy chairman of Krupps, for instance, expressed his appreciation for the cooperation shown in the establishment of the new factories, and looked forward to happy years of association with Cymru Newydd. The deputy Gauleiter of Byelorussia, on an official visit to the Protectorate, was brought in one day, and various high-ranking officers of SS and Wermacht clicked their heels and saluted. Photographers were always to hand to record such visits, and once a party of American journalists came, from the sizeable US press corps which had remained in London ever since the surrender.

'I'm part-Welsh myself,' said one of these correspondents. 'My mother's name was Harrington – that's a Welsh name isn't it? Maybe when you're settled back in Cimry I can come down and do another piece, and maybe find out where my folks are from.'

'You would be more than welcome to visit Cymru,' said the Llyw-Elect, 'which is pronounced, incidentally,

43

as though it were spelt Cumry in English – the orthography of our language being derived, as you are no doubt aware, both from the Latin and from altogether separate Celto-Sanskrit roots. We Welsh have always prided ourselves upon our hospitality, and I shall see to it that this ancient tradition is more than honoured in Cymru Newydd. *Croeso*, as we say in Welsh, welcome indeed at any time!'

Nice guy, the Americans thought him. Maybe the Krauts were doing something right at last.

4 *Free meals and assurances*

No visitors had yet been invited, though, to visit Cymru Newydd itself. It was not that there was anything to hide. By and large the Welsh of all kinds accepted the situation calmly, if not gratefully. There was a lot to be said for it. The English had all gone, leaving many houses and cottages vacant for the Returnees; the newly-built huts were plain but serviceable; the spanking prefabricated munition factories gave a promise of universal employment for the first time since the war. In the meantime everyone was given free meals, at communal kitchens, which were no worse than the rations everyone else was subsisting on. The University of Wales no longer existed, but the local schools were still operating, and their teachers were delighted to be told that Welsh-language tuition would henceforth be compulsory for all ages.

Movement within Cymru Newydd, it was true, was severely restricted, but hardly more so than in Britain as a whole, and the German administrators, from the Reich-Inviter down, were one and all anxious to reassure the people that they were there only to help, merely holding the country in trust, as it were, until the arrival of their Llyw and the establishment of Cymru Newydd in the full glory of its sovereignty. 'C-Day is near! *Der Tag*! We shall all rejoice then.'

5 *Some were not happy with the arrangements, though*

Among the minority who were not happy with the arrangements were Sir Gwilym Adam-Jones and his wife Miriam. They had been allocated a fairly poky terrace cottage in Machynlleth, the putative capital of Cymru Newydd, and they badly missed the perks and privileges that Oxford college heads expected even then – wines hidden away in cellars, the odd pheasant slipped in from college estates. Although they had both made good use of their Welshness down the years, they had never been Welsh Nationalists: on the contrary, they were (especially Miriam) the very epitome of what cynics called Establishment Welsh, young patriot bloods called Uncle Toms, and Lord Brackenthorpe called Kitchen Taffies. Now they much regretted defining themselves as Welsh on their census forms, and resented the new fame of that not particularly distinguished specialist in medieval Celtic poesy, that prime common-room bore, Llywelyn Parry-Morris.

During the idle days of waiting, the Adam-Joneses gathered around them a little group of similar

45

dissidents, most of them hostile to Parry-Morris on old academic grounds, some because they thought he was behaving no better than a Quisling, and others again simply because they resented his pretensions. There were several university lecturers, for instance. There were a few members of landed county families, proud enough of their heritage to have declared themselves Welsh and consequently dragged in from their crumbled manor houses. There was a handful of conservative gentlemen-farmers and their embittered wives, anciently Welsh but long Anglicized. These people met over acorn coffee and biscuits in the Adam-Joneses' chilly front parlour (which Miriam had nevertheless managed to dignify, somehow or other, with a picture of Their Majesties the ex-King and Queen during a long-ago visit to Jesus College, and a large oil painting of Sir Gwilym, in full academic rig, commissioned by the college to commemorate his 25 years in office).

Miriam thought of the little coterie as her salon, and presided over it very grandly, but the conversation nearly always settled down to the subject of the Llyw-Designate. 'The little squirt,' one of the squires would say, 'what does he know about Wales anyway? Whoever heard of him before now? Did you ever hear of him, Robert? I never heard of him.' Or: 'I can tell you, I didn't fight in that bloody war just to split up the United Kingdom for a lot of damned nationalists.' Or: 'What does he know about dipping sheep or bovine tuberculosis? Why wasn't he in the Army, anyway?' Or: 'We knew the Parry-Morrises long ago. They were nobody much, just tenant farmers with a clever-clever son. The Morrises came from Llanystumdwy way, I think. The Parrys were Merioneth people. Nobody much.' Or: 'I can't think, Sir Gwilym, why the Germans didn't think of inviting you to do the job, somebody distinguished like you, somebody we could all respect and look up to.' 'Because he wouldn't do it,' said Miriam, 'that's why. Because he's a true Briton, not a wretched little Welsh Nat collaborator. Oh, I could wring that man's neck.' And she did wring it, in an imaginary gesture of great ferocity.

'Be that as it may, my dear,' said grand Sir Gwilym, 'we must restrain our anger for our own sakes. Nevertheless wild horses will not drag me to the station to greet him on his arrival – not if Adolf Hitler himself commanded it.' And on that they were all agreed.

HOMECOMING

1 *The Llyw comes home*

When the time came, though, they one and all stood among the serried ranks which waited to greet Y Llyw in the station yard at Machynlleth. This is because large official notices all over town had ordered them to be there, under pain of the possible penalties prescribed by Protectorate Law 2607. 'What are the possible penalties prescribed by Law 2607?' several people asked old William Ellis, who had been a High Court judge in the old days. He had never heard of Law 2607, of course – who had? – but did not like to admit it. 'The penalities,' he said, 'are unspecified,' and there he was right.

Although they did not know it, this was their last day of liberty. The factories were now all ready to start production; job allocations had been completed; the old Parliament House in Machynlleth, where the rebel Owain Glyndŵr had supposedly called his assembly in 1404, had been prepared as headquarters for the Llyw, and down the road the former mansion of the Marquis of Londonderry had been refurbished as the Reich-Legation to the National Home of Cymru Newydd, soon to be occupied by Heinrich Schinkel (his office of Reich-Inviter being now defunct). The Press, including correspondents from several foreign countries, had been brought to Machynlleth in a convoy of buses, and were now assembled on a dais on the station platform to await the arrival of the Llyw's train. Schinkel was there too, in his new diplomatic uniform. So was a small covey of black-breeched and booted SS officers. So was Lord Brackenthorpe, and the former Cowley Works Brass Band. The Welsh men, women and children marshalled in the yard outside had all been given plastic daffodils, made as a fraternal gesture by fellow-citizens in the Protectorate of Bohemia.

The train that brought Parry-Morris into his kingdom was a very special one. For one thing it was drawn by a steam locomotive with a large Welsh dragon on the front of its boiler. For another, it consisted only of a single Pullman carriage, with vases of daffodils at every window. 'I could wish,' the Llyw had said, 'that they had been leeks, in honour of our immemorial custom on this day,' but he had been persuaded by the Ministry of Propaganda experts that the daffodil was more readily recognized, around the world, as a national emblem of Wales. 'Then I shall wear the leek myself,' and so he did, largely pinned to the collar of his blue overcoat. 'Then I shall wear it too,' said the Gauleiter, and he had a larger one still attached to the chest of his black uniform. 'We are brothers in the New Europe,' he said to Parry-Morris, and together they disembarked from the train and walked down the station platform to the strains of *Men of Harlech* from the Brass Band.

'One moment, Herr Gauleiter, if you please,' said Parry-Morris, and he walked over to the band's conductor to shake his hand. 'You played at the beginning of the Great Return,' said the Llyw, 'how proper that you should be playing again at its completion.'

'It's very good of you to say so, Doctor,' said the conductor, 'the boys will be very gratified – and the girls too, as you see we have several female trumpeters and Mrs Thomas there is brilliant on the tuba. And if I may venture to say so, the best of luck in your great task.'

'Thank you, thank you dear friend,' said Parry-Morris, reaching out to grasp the hand of the conductor, who hastily transferred his baton to the other.

2 *A message from the Führer*

'And now for the great moment,' said the Gauleiter, 'the moment of your personal triumph, and your national fulfilment.' Out they went into the station yard, and at that moment *Land of Our Fathers* blared out from the platform behind them. A field of yellow nodded in front, as the crowd of Welsh people waved their daffodils and broke into the words of the great anthem. Tears ran down the Llyw's cheeks. Even the Gauleiter later confessed himself moved, and several people said they had known nothing like it since one of the great international rugby matches at Cardiff Arms Park before the war. The anthem was succeeded by a wave of cheering and whistling, until at last von Harden raised his hand for silence.

'People of Wales,' he said, 'fellow-citizens of the new Europe, fellow-workers for the future of our continent and the glory of our common cause, your day

50

has arrived. After so many centuries of cruel oppression and frustration, on this glorious St David's Day you are to become an independent sovereign people as you were in the days of old. Your days of suffering are over. Cimry – er, Cymru, is Cymru again – Cymru Newydd, New Wales, an honoured self-governing homeland in the new Europe. Today I bring you greetings from the Protectorate Government. More than that, I bring you greetings from the Europe-Führer himself, who has watched with pride and paternal interest the preparations for this day. Here is what our Führer says' – and unfolding with great deliberation a paper handed him by one of his aides, he put on his glasses and read as follows: "Welsh men and women! Welcome to your destiny. Put the past behind you. Redeem yourselves and your national honour by work and dedication. We shall be watching you with care and attention, mindful of your responsibilities to our common struggle. *Seig Heil*!' And it is signed, personally, Adolf Hitler.'

'*Seig Heil*!' then cried the Gauleiter himself, standing at the salute. '*Seig Heil*!' cried Schinken and all the officers. '*Seig Heil*!' murmured Lord Brackenthrope, rather sheepishly. But Parry-Morris was busily blowing his nose, and when behind their backs the band launched itself once more into *Hen Wlad fy Nhadau*, the people standing in the forecourt sang with it, tentatively at first, defiantly at the end.

The Gauleiter raised his hand for silence again. 'And now,' he said, 'at this grand moment of your national history, it is my honour and privilege to present to you, on behalf of the Protectorate Government and of the

Führer. 'your own Llyw, who will assume from this moment the duties of leader of the Welsh nation.' He flung out his hand in the direction of Parry-Morris, who looked fixedly into the sky as though his mind were on higher things. 'Will you have this man, this famous scholar, this unwavering patriot, this great Welshman, to be your leader?' The crowds, not knowing how best to respond, murmured incoherently and shuffled its feet (only Miriam Adam-Jones, near the back, uttered a very audible 'No, we jolly well won't'), so the Gauleiter proceeded anyway.

'Very well then, Dr Llywelyn Parry-Morris, by virtue of my authority as head of the Protectorate Government in Great Britain, and as plenipotentiary of the Europe-Führer, Adolf Hitler, I now declare you Llyw of Cymru Newydd, the National Homeland of the Welsh people.' The band played again. The Gauleiter pinned to Parry-Morris's coat, beside the leek, an enamel Welsh dragon.

3 *'What a load of balls'*

The crowd dispersed. The big-wigs, German, English and Welsh, adjourned to walk in loose procession to the old Parliament House for the formalities which would officially establish Cymru Newydd.

'A great day for you, what, Parry-Morris?' remarked Lord Brackenthorpe breezily as they walked up from the station. 'Just for a moment I thought they might say they wanted Barabbas after all! No, just kidding. You've waited for this long enough, haven't you?'

'For nearly 800 years,' said Parry-Morris, 'since the tragic day when on the bridge over the River Irfon our Last Leader, *Ein Llyw Olaf*, died at the hands of a brutal English trooper, subjecting us ever thereafter, with the exception of the glorious years of national revival under the the aegis of the great Owain Glyndŵr, whom I am proud to count among my own forbears on my mother's side, the Parrys of Trawsfynydd being colaterally descended, by way of the Vaughans of Ystrad Cemlyn, from the house of Sycharth – as I was saying, except for those exhilarating years of rebellion, subject ever since to the unjust and aloof government of you English.'

'What a load of balls,' was all Lord Brackenthorpe replied, moving away to join the Gauleiter.

'A load of balls! I could not help overhearing you,' said von Harden, 'and admiring as always your vivid and virile use of idiom. It is true that our Welsh friends do sometimes indulge themselves in, how can I put it, a certain tendency towards hyperbole.'

'Verbal diarrhoea, we used to call it in the British Army of blessed memory,' said Brackenthorpe, 'but you'll soon be putting an end to all that, won't you?'

The Gauleiter smiled faintly. 'I believe the Führer is anxious that the Homeland should above all be productive and disciplined in the cause – as you know, we expect it to undertake a substantial proportion of small arms ammunition production for our armies on the eastern front. I don't suppose there will be much time for hyperbole.'

For the moment, all the same, hyperbole was everywhere. Attended always by officials and military men, cameramen and reporters, Gauleiter and Llyw went through the necessary formalities, signing papers, exchanging signatures, shaking hands for the photographers, drinking toasts, sitting down to lunch at Schinkel's Legation, ceremonially raising the Welsh flag above the old Paliament House, before, as evening set in, the visitors drove away in their fleets of limousines and buses, and Parry-Morris was left as undisputed Llyw of Cymru Newydd.

'All codswallop,' said Lord Brackenthorpe to the Gauleiter as they drove through the frontier posts on their way to Oxford. It was true that the Llyw's quarters, a shabby complex at the back of the Parliament House, were rather less than presidential, their single ceremonial feature being a high-backed Eisteddfod chair presented to some long-forgotten poet at Cefn-y-Waun in 1912; and that very evening notices appeared everywhere in Cymru Newydd ordering the entire population to report for work allocation at 6.30 next morning.

4 *A word of advice from the Reich-Legate*

'We all much admired that little demonstration of national pride this morning,' said Schinkel to Parry-Morris before they parted that night, 'when so many of your fellow-countrymen seemed a trifle reluctant to hail the Führer – perfectly understandable on this particular day of celebration. You yourself, I noticed, were quite overcome by your emotions! But if I might – what is it the English say? – tip the wink a little,

54

I think it might be wiser in future if you encouraged your people to show a more real gratitude towards the Protectorate Government and our generous Führer.'

IMPLEMENTATION

1 *What citizenship meant in practice*

'Do you read me?' Schinkel might have added that evening, for neither he nor the Gauleiter, nor any of their officials, were altogether sure how much Parry-Morris understood about the nature of the Dimension, or for that matter the nature of the Homeland. 'One must be careful of those Welsh monkeys,' the Führer himself had told Goebbels, who had passed on the warning to von Harden, 'they are sly and devious, not to be trusted. I have had a very peculiar feeling in my bones about them, ever since that snake Lloyd-George came to see me at Berchtesgarten – all smiles and flattery, but he was the very man who had stabbed us in the back in the first war, depriving us of our righteous victory, condemning us to wicked humiliations until we of the Party restored Germany to its rightful place. That's the Welsh for you. Scum. Serpents.' On the line to Oxford Goebbels did a very fair impersonation of the Führer declaiming this message, and ironically, despite himself, von Harden thought he sounded a little like Parry-Morris . . .

Anyway, very soon the people of Cymru Newydd discovered what citizenship of their Homeland meant in practice. All contact with the rest of the world was now ended. 'Just what you wanted, Llyw, is it not?' said Schinkel mischievously. 'Absolute lack of contamination from the Anglo-American culture?' The high guarded barrier surrounded the entire area, with dogs and watchtowers; radios and televisions were forbidden; the only newspaper was Y Cymro Rhydd, the Free Welshman, a weekly sheet produced by staff from the Propaganda Ministry. The public signs, almost all prohibitions, which quickly appeared everywhere were in Welsh and German, and so were all commands. Although more than half the citizenry was monoglot English, necessity soon made everyone fluent in elementary Welsh at last. The Welsh Homeland, in short, was becoming a reality – Welsh in population, Welsh in language, Welsh in leadership.

There was not much time though for patriotic satisfaction. The Homeland also soon revealed itself to be one huge work-camp, its several factories working around the clock to produce the simpler forms of munitions. Living conditions were harsher now; rations got sparser as the months went by; old and young, men and women, were given their labour tasks, and the shifts paraded for their work, morning and evening, beneath the twin flags of the swastika and the red dragon. Parry Morris was always there, every day, twice a day, to exhort them with some apt quotation from a Welsh praise poet. 'My friends,' he would cry, 'the way may be hard and the sacrifice cruel, but what we are doing today will be remembered with pride and gratitude by our descendants, free proud Welsh citizens, until the end of history. *Cymru am Byth*! – Wales for Ever!' – and there would be a resentful murmur of response as the workers shuffled off to their labours.

'That oaf,' Miriam would mutter as she made for her lathe, fastening her headscarf, 'How I would love to murder him. If this is the New Wales, give me purgatory every time' – and all around here there would be a stirring of agreement. The most fervently patriotic of the citizens, who welcomed the compulsory use of Welsh, and sang the national anthem with unfailing passion even on shivery evenings in the drizzle, began to see Parry-Morris as at best a buffoon, at worst a traitor. He was greeted with cat-calls sometimes, as he moved around the camps and factories.

2 *Yet the Llyw bore himself grandly*

He was unconcerned by these discontents, and totally ignored the catcalls. Although it was obvious that the Germans had complete ultimate control of the Homeland, and Schinkel did not hide his authority, the Llyw bore himself ever more grandly as the head of a sovereign State. Crests emblazoned his offices. Flags flew always above them. He demanded, and got, a formal guard of *Plant Owain*, 'Owen's Children,' named after Welsh guerillas of the Middle Ages. He arranged a uniform for himself, to be worn on formal occasions: derived from the costume of the Archdruid at the pre-war National Eisteddfods, it was a druidical garb of blue and orange, with a great golden torque (made of cardboard, alas) protecting the Llyw's chest.

He had Welsh currency notes cyclostyled, to be the only legal tender within the Homeland, and crude Welsh ink-stamps made to frank the official communications and censored printed cards which were all that was left to post. He drew up a legal code for Cymru Newydd, owing nothing to the English Common Law, but looking back, as he said, to the ancient Welsh codes of the great Hywel Dda.

The Germans humoured him. They swapped jokes about him in the Protectorate mess, and sent photographs of him in his Druidical gear home to entertain their families. Schinkel sent one too, just for fun, to Lord Brackenthorpe. 'The Llyw in his native habitat,' he wrote on the back, and Brackenthorpe replied on behalf of the Associate Government with an entertaining limerick:

> We've heard some preposterous tales,
> Crossing the border from Wales.
> But do let us know –
> It worries us so –
> Do Llyws have feathers, or scales?

3 *On style in Cymru Newydd*

'This is not a concentration camp,' as Schinkel sometimes said laughingly to the Llyw, 'such as you may have read about in the papers': and indeed the Homeland was in most ways genuinely autonomous. Parry-Morris really was its Leader, and his authority was more than mere show. The Germans were happy to give him control over most of the Homeland's internal affairs, and he himself built up a substantial staff to deal with the work. Against all his inclinations Sir Gwilym Adam-Jones became his Chief Clerk, and arranged a secretarial job too for his daughter Angharad ('Darlings how could you?' demanded Miriam. 'Where needs must be . . .' sighed Sir Gwilym, omitting to mention that life at the Llyw's headqarters was a great deal more civilized than life in a munitions plant).

The office was run with great formality. Past the *Plant Owain* sentries one went into a reception area where a stern Welshman (formerly headmaster of Ebbw Wale Intermediate School) demanded one's business: through a room-full of busy clerks, including Angharad, to wait for a moment kicking one's heels in an ante-room until Sir Gwilym appeared to take one into the Llyw's private office. 'Good morning, good morning,' Parry-Morris would affably cry (in Welsh of course) rising from his desk with outstretched hand, and after an exchange of courtesies, and perhaps a quotation or two of medieval poesy, business would begin.

Only three over-riding regulations governed the Llyw's independence of action. First, the maintenance of the closed border was in the hands of the Germans. Secondly, the food supply was beyond his control. Thirdly, and most importantly, it was made clear to him that the very existence of Cymru Newydd depended upon the maintenance of production from the arms factories. 'We are doing our best for Wales. You must in return do your best for the New Europe.'

Parry-Morris performed his duties with panache. His

style became ever more confident and flamboyant. 'In the days of the Welsh princes,' he used to say, 'it was the pride of the *uchelwyr*, the landed gentry, to treat the commonality with equal courtesy, to share with them the pleasures of their table and their entertainment, and to make them feel that they were not mere serfs or tenants, but partners in the comradeship of Wales. So shall it be in Cymru Newydd.' Whoever came into his office, be it the Reich-Legate or some slatternly woman demanding sick leave, Parry-Morris's responses were identically polite. He would offer them a cup of elderflower tea – 'not tea as we remember it, but at least made from authentically Welsh ingredients.' He would speak of the grand progress being made towards genuine independence – congratulate applicants upon their progress in the Welsh language, if they were New Speakers (as learners were called) – tell them a tale or two about the glory days of Owain Glyndwr or Llywelyn ap Gruffydd – and then settle down to the matter in hand.

Sometimes he made a tour of his domain. The Germans gave him an allocation of methane for his old Humber (left behind by the Marquis of Londonderry), and Sir Gwilym Adam-Jones acted as his chauffeur (Miriam: 'How can you bring yourself to do it?' Sir Gwilym: 'Ah well, my dear, it gets me out of the office!') With a couple of *Plant* in the back seat they would trundle rather slowly around Cymru Newydd, bumpily over the unkempt and potholed roads, with a red dragon ensign fluttering on each front mudguard, and deputations of local worthies to greet them with flags and loyal posters at every town. '*Gyfeillion*,' the

Llyw would begin his speech everywhere, 'my friends, did we ever suppose – nay, did we ever dream in our wildest dreams? – that we would meet in these circumstances, beneath our beloved flag, in our own dear country free at last?' And so they would enter the factory, to inspect the production graphs.

4 *Too large for his boots?*

'I wonder, Sir,' said Schinkel musingly to the Gauleiter, during one of the latter's regular visits, 'if we are giving him rather too much encouragement? It strikes me sometimes that he is getting – what is the English idiom? – rather too large for his boots.'

'Let him be, Schinkel,' said von Harden. 'Another Anglo-Saxon saying is: "If it be not broke, do not mend it." Cymru Newydd is proceeding admirably, thanks very largely, I may say, to your own tact and insight. All your dispatches have been passed on directly to the Führer, and he has repeatedly expressed himself satisfied with progress, especially since we were able to report last month that 7.92mm ammunition had passed the ten million mark. I am told he is greatly amused by the antics of our Last Leader – I hear he once suggested, purely in his characteristic fun of course, that Parry-Morris ought to be sent to the Russian front, to take over operations there! So rest assured, dear Schinkel, our eyes, like yours, are firmly on the Llyw, and if he ever does over-step the mark, *pfft* . . . As it is, just let things ride, my dear fellow.'

'Thank you, Gauleiter, I am much obliged. But the

Führer does realize, does he not, that the ten million production figure is unlikely to be repeated? The work force is already beginning to weaken, as we always foresaw, and very soon we shall have to start shipping people off to Eryri.'

'To the Ultimate Homeland, you mean? Have you discussed that matter with Parry-Morris?'

'I have suggested that we might make it a kind of inner shrine of Welshness, a sort of Valhalla perhaps, or a residence of honour not unlike the Forbidden City in China. He was much taken with the idea, and told me at some length about the particular significance of the mountains of Eryri as the heartland of the Welsh meaning – princes – bards – legends – you know the kind of thing. I suggested that perhaps in the fullness of time he might wish to retire there himself.'

'Oh, Schinkel, you naughty man. What a rogue you are, what a scamp!'

LINGUISTICS

1 *Little gnomes in the mountains*

For some months matters went well enough, if drearily, in the Homeland. The situation was this. Both the United States and Japan had remained neutral in the war. Almost the whole of Europe was under Hitler's rule in one way or the other, but the conflict with Russia dragged on, year after year, the German and Russian armies having fought each other into stagnation with prodigious waste of men and munitions on either side. Their resources of manpower were now about even, and the crucial factor was thus the production of arms and ammunition.

The Führer enlarged upon this one day at a pan-European conference of Gauleiters in Germania. It was during a break in the formal discussions, and the Gauleiters eagerly crowded around him, senior ones closest to the presence, as they took a break in the Chancellory gardens.

'Fortunately we have,' Hitler told them, 'an almost bottomless fount of labour to produce our military necessities for us. It is like a gift from God! Think of it, all those millions of sub-humans and neo-humans and un-humans, from the Atlantic to the Crimea, given us by destiny to be our slaves! Ha ha, it is like the gnomes in *Das Rheingold*, isn't it? Remember Alberich renouncing love? Remember the giants' theme – *pom, pom, pom pom*?' – and he conducted an imaginary orchestra with passionate gusto, stamping his feet at the same time. 'Ah, what the gods have given us Germans, what we owe to destiny, a destiny that we must ourselves grasp and bend to our purposes!'

'And that reminds me, von Harden' – the Gauleiter of Great Britain was always close at his side – 'how about those Welsh swine of yours? Are you bending them properly to our purposes? I haven't heard much about them lately. You must make the most of them, Gauleiter, while the going is good – we shall never run out of Slavs, but Jews are getting a bit short already.'

'They are as industrious as the *nibelung*,' von Harden obsequiously assured him, 'just like so many little gnomes in their mountains, and as it happens, *mein Führer*, we are planning a press visit of neutral diplomats and journalists to show the world the benevolent progress we have made with their national independence.'

'Ha ha,' said Hitler. 'Excellent. I'll see that one of my Ministers shows up too. And what is the production rate of these gnomes?'

'The highest among all the *untermensch*. For one thing their rations have so far been relatively high (although of course that won't last), and for another we have had the useful cooperation of their own leader, the inestimable Parry-Morris, who is still leading his people energetically into their Promised Land.'

'Perhaps we should give him a medal, while there is still time.'

'Oh he would never accept one, *mein Feuhrer*. You forget he is the head of a sovereign State! He is much more likely to suggest giving a medal to you!'

'And I would accept it! Von Harden, you must tell him from me that the Führer would be honoured to accept it! What would it be called?'

'Oh, the Order of the Red Dragon, or the Order of Merlin, or some such nonsense. He'd pin it on your chest and embrace you and spout a lot of unintelligible compliments in a language nobody understands.'

'What a lark,' Hitler concluded, as they returned to the conference hall, 'to be embraced by the living dead, in a language that will soon be as dead as the dodo itself. Not in our lifetime, my friends, but in our children's, German will be the universal tongue.'

2 *Who would have thought it?*

Dr Parry-Morris was of another mind. Over the months he introduced a very contradictory series of orders concerning the language of the homeland. Welsh was now to be the one official language, and German would be used only under compulsion. 'We are one people in Cymru Newydd,' he declared, 'we do not need two languages, and he took to professing complete ignorance of German in conversation with his patrons.

Who would have thought it? Even Lady Adam-Jones grudgingly approved. 'I suppose we've got to live with his silly tin-pot Welsh, but I'm damned if I'm going to start talking German.' Angharad was pleased too, if only because her boy friend Emrys Owen, a pupil of the Llyw's at Oxford, though born and brought up in Surrey, had developed over time into a fiery Welsh patriot. Sir Gwilym reserved judgement on the matter.

He remembered well, he said, coming up against Parry-Morris in the little matter of the Welsh grace which had traditionally been spoken in Hall on St David's Day. As everyone in the college then discovered, linguistics brought out the obdurate in the man.

3 *Obduracy of the man*

The Llyw can hardly have been surprised when the Reich-Legate tackled him about it. 'There is a little matter I would like to discuss with you, Llyw' (Schinkel generally called Parry-Morris 'Llyw,' as a matter of courtesy).

'By all means, Legate' (Parry-Morris generally called Schinkel 'Legate' as a matter of etiquette).

'It concerns language,' said Schinkel. 'I am disturbed to see that your recent official notices have been promulgated – that is the word? 'promulgated'?'

'Very likely,' said Parry-Morris carelessly. 'I am not familiar with every nuance of the English language, inasmuch as it possesses nuances – in Cymraeg we call it *yr iaith fain*, the thin language. But 'promulgated' sounds correct to me, if you are referring to the publication or display of my official announcements. What disturbs you about them?'

'They are promulgated, published and displayed only in Welsh.'

'And?'

'And, Llyw, I would wish them to be promulgated, published or displayed also in the language of the

Protecting Power, in the language of the new Europe, in the language of the agency, in short, which has by the exertion of its benign will brought your Cymru Newydd into existence.'

Parry-Morris was busying himself with something on his desk, and appeared to be taking no notice. Schinkel rapped his desk with his swagger-stick.

'Do you hear me, Llyw?'

Parry-Morris laid down his papers, leant back in his Eisteddfod chair of 1912 and removed his spectacles.

'I do indeed hear you, Legate, and I am astonished by what I hear. Nay, I am perturbed, horrified – *brawychu* as we say in Welsh , which by the way – I don't know if I've ever told you – we prefer to call *Yr Hen Iaith*, the Old Language, recognizing its seniority among the living literary languages of Europe, with the possible exception of the Greek – although as you will be well aware, Legate, being of a literary turn yourself, and having if I remember correctly served your country among the Hellenes too, there are very considerable differences between the demotic Greek of today and the language of Sophocles, Demosthenes, or even of later scholars and poets such as Callimachus.'

'What are you talking about? What has this to do with your promulgations? Stop this nonsense, Llyw.'

'Stop this nonsense! Oh Colonel Schinkel, I never thought to hear you express yourself in such crude terms. Ours has been a relationship, I have always supposed, characterized not only by courtesies of an older kind, but also by a degree of subtlety. It was expressly our agreement, was it not, since the start of Cymru Newydd, that ours was to be a sovereign State, albeit only a fragment in the great pattern of Europe, and necessarily subject to the patronage of the occupying Power.

'Now what, Colonel Schinkel, is the first attribute of a sovereign State? No, Legate, do not answer me – I speak rhetorically. You would no doubt suggest racial purity, and I admit it is an arguable viewpoint. I, however, would reply – *language*! In your philosophies, sir, nobody can become a German – you are a German, or an Aryan anyway, or you are not. In my philosophy, and in the philosophy of this little brotherhood of ours, anybody can be Welsh who is willing to become Welsh – and the badge of the commitment, the tie which will one day make a true brotherhood of us all within the wider fraternity of a free Europe of the nations, is our language, the noble language of our ancestors, our poets down the centuries. That is why, Reich-Legate, Cymraeg is the medium of my *promulgations*.'

'And why is there no German too?'

The Llyw looked at him in a silence that was more pitying than contemptuous. Schinkel felt oddly obliged to shift his feet.

'And now, Herr Legate, if you will excuse me, I have the duties of my office to attend to. My Chief of Protocol will see you out': and when he rang the big brass handbell on his desk, a suddenly-promoted Sir Gwilym appeared from the outer office to escort the Legate to the yard – where at least, Schinkel was relieved to note, the swastika still flew on its flagpole beside the Red Dragon.

PRESENTATION

1 *No names, no packdrill*

On the whole they maintained the proprieties. Parry-Morris never did give way on the language question, and often intervened when he heard English spoken among his citizens. 'Shut up you old fraud,' said one of those young Oxford dons when he found himself rebuked in this way, 'we're not your bloody pupils, you know, nor your subjects either.'

'You'd better be careful talking like that,' said his friend, 'or you'll get on Schinkel's report list.'

'He wouldn't dare,' said the young don, but he looked thoughtful all the same.

For it was clear to all that the Llyw, despite his displays of obduracy, was not unfriendly with the Legate. 'I render unto Caesar,' he used to say in his booming voice, 'the things which are Caesar's,' but just what he meant by the quotation, in the context of Cymru Newydd, was uncertain. Schinkel, for his part, generally left well alone. His dispatches to Oxford and Germania were blithe and optimistic. As he told the Gauleiter, it was in everyone's interests that for the moment at least the Homeland should function without unnecessary minor unpleasantnesses. 'I believe they used to have a saying in the British Army, 'No names, no packdrill'.'

'Oh I do so agree, Schinkel – but 'No names, no

packdrill',' the Gauleiter laughed, 'what pithy sayings the English do have.'

2 *An unexpectedly important visitor*

One reason von Harden did not wish to upset the applecart – 'Upset the applecart! Marvellous! Another for my collection!' – was that his Propaganda and Enlightenment Secretary in Oxford, on express instructions from Germania, had now arranged the grand summer visitation of neutral diplomats, journalists and Red Cross representatives. They called it a 'presentation.' The most influential of the visitors would be Americans, and the occasion would be a supreme opportunity to present a benevolent German image in the United States, and influence wavering liberal opinion there. For years rumours, no more, had circulated about concentration and extermination camps in Poland and the east. The Propaganda Ministry declared these too to be no more than ethnic homelands for Jews, Gypsies, Poles and other nationalities, to which foreign observers could unfortunately not be invited because of dangerous conditions near the Russian front. Cymru Newydd on the other hand, said the Ministry, was perfectly peaceful, and was normally closed to outsiders only by the wishes of its own inhabitants, who preferred to establish their Homeland without external interference – they had, after all, suffered from almost a thousand years of English intervention.

The visitors would find a people well on the way to

nationhood, with their own leaders and their own values, speaking their own language under the friendly auspices of the Euro-Reich. This was a true expression of the New Order. It was the way all Europe was going. Although unhappily, no accommodation was available within the Homeland of a suitable standard for distinguished strangers – Cymru Newydd was a small and struggling nation – a full day would be devoted to the visit, and the visitors would be flown from London to the German military airfield at Oswestry, close to the frontier of Cymru Newydd, where cars would meet them.

What was their surprise to find, not simply Gauleiter von Harden there to greet them, and Legate Schinkel, and a group of smiling officials from the Propaganda Ministry, but none other than Josef Goebbels himself, one of the great men of the Nazi hierarchy, waiting smiling on the tarmac as they clambered out of their Junkers 55 on a lovely summer morning! 'I am not your guide,' he laughed as they crowded around him. 'I am a visitor too! I have never been here before. But the Führer was especially anxious that I should welcome you to this happy little enterprise of ours, and besides, I thought it a nice opportunity to see it for myself, to make sure that all is going as we would wish it to go, and in particular to meet its redoubtable leader, Dr Parry-Morris – called in his own language, am I not right Schinkel, Y Llyw? Am I saying it right, Schinkel? You must be fluent by now. For myself, gentlemen – oh, and ladies too, I'm delighted to see some representatives of the fair sex among you – I cannot claim any mastery of the Welsh tongue. And I dare say that goes for you too!'

All laughed dutifully, and so with general bonhomie they were bundled into their cars and were driven through the frontier posts – 'note the flags!' – into Cymru Newydd.

3 *No questions now*

Dr Parry-Morris was there to greet them at the door of his headquarters, Adam-Jones at his side, and he did it in Welsh. 'Bravo,' said Goebbels, who received the brunt of this greeting. 'I am reminded' – and he turned now to the admiring audience of neutrals – 'of a fine poem by the English poet Robert Graves – English, Parry-Morris? I rather fear so – in which some strange and unidentified creatures crawl out of the sea at some Welsh beach or other. They were greeted by the local Mayor, so the poet says, as I remember it, 'in English and in fluent Welsh.' I remember so well the enunciation of Foreign Minister Ambassador Ribbentrop when he quoted the poem to me in the course of one of our discussions about the Homeland – 'in English and in flew-ent Welsh.' 'Flew-ent Welsh' – that's how he said it! Such an entertaining colleague, our Ribbentrop.'

The Llyw was not much amused. He had always disliked the poem, which he thought a mockery of Welsh culture. So he merely returned a distant smile, and led the party into the courtyard, where tea and Welsh oatcakes, *bara brith*, had been laid out for them on trestle tables, and was served by a team of Welshwomen under the command of Miriam Adam-

Jones ('Hardly a feast, is it?' she murmured to some of the plumper Americans, 'but in case you've forgotten, there's a war on . . .')

'Welcome to Cymru Newydd,' the Llyw now proclaimed loudly – in English. 'I am proud to welcome you to a Wales, however truncated, that is governing its own affairs for the first time since 1282, or possibly since 1404, and sorry to have to address you not in our own language but in English, which we Welsh have been accustomed to call *Yr Iaith Fain*, the Thin Language, owing to its relative paucity of idiom. But there we are, my friends, I have a feeling that, with the possible exception of Reich-Minister Goebbels himself, you are not *flew-ent* in Welsh!' (Loud laughter, much of it from Goebbels).

'Welcome anyway. Your visit is a celebration for us – our very first chance to show ourselves to the world at large. I am the Llyw, what you might call the President of our little country, and this is Sir Gwilym Adam-Jones, a distinguished academic and my Chief of Protocol and Administration.' (Sir Gwilym, s*otto voce*: 'First I've heard of it'). 'Please talk to anyone you like, and go wherever you wish in our small community, subject of course only to restrictions of security. And now, ladies and gentlemen, if you have any questions before we, as it were, let you loose . . .?'

But here von Harden intervened. 'No questions now, Llyw, I think. Let us hand over our guests to their guides from the Propaganda and Enlightenment Ministry – we don't want them to get lost! – and perhaps we shall have time for questions at the end of their tour.' So the visitors, shepherded in groups and supplied with shiny brochures entitled *An Experiment in Pride*, smiled their thanks to Parry-Morris and were taken on their tour. They walked around Machynlleth, they were taken in coaches to Dolgellau and Llanidloes, they were whisked through busy factories, they peered into living blocks and cottage billets, they were shown, in the distance, the mountains of Eryri where, they were told, there would eventually be a national retirement home for honoured citizens – an innovation already introduced in other autonomous regions of Reich-Europe. They did not have much chance to talk to the inhabitants, being told that few of them spoke any English, but they were treated to a short concert of Welsh folk-songs.

There was no denying that the people of the new Wales looked rather thin. 'Aren't they a trifle skinny?,' the correspondent of the Chicago *Sun* remarked to his minder. The minder shrugged.

'They live on workers' rations, and as you know, in these times of war, food is not plentiful. Their rations are carefully measured and distributed.'

'By the Cymru Government?'

'By the Protectorate Government, which naturally retains ultimate authority over the allocation of resources – Cymru Newydd is, of course, only a self-governing province of Reich-Europe'

'Well, they look a bit too skinny to me,' said the Chicago *Sun*, but so clean was everything they saw, so hard were the workers evidently working, so efficient appeared to be the hospital – 'staffed by the very best surgeons from the old Welsh health service' – that he put it out of his mind. 'Observe the red dragon flags,' said the man from the Propaganda Ministry.

4 'This is all a great charade'

In the meantime Dr Goebbels had taken the Llyw aside for a private chat – just the two of us, he said, dismissing Gauleiter, Legate and all the minions, and withdrawing into Parry-Morris's private office.

'Now, Parry-Morris,' said Goebbels the moment they were inside the door. 'Let us cut the cackle, as I am told the Americans say, and get down to business. This is all a great charade, is it not? I know it, and I think you know it. You are no more the head of a sovereign State than I am Mickey Mouse, and I am disturbed to hear that you sometimes seem to forget the fact. What is this foolishness about no German on your notices? What is this about stamps and paper currency? Have you no respect for the Reich and our Führer?'

The Llyw moved to his own side of the table and sat down. 'Do please be seated, Reich-Minister. Don't stand upon ceremony. We Welsh are an unceremonious people, and we certainly hold no store by personal formality. But there is an old saying in our language that the crow is white to his neighbours, meaning you see that among our people, as far back as the beginning of recorded history, there have been generally acknowledged principles of social equality which, now that we have at last re-achieved our sovereign condition, we naturally interpret as implying political equality too. I have made it perfectly clear to both the Gauleiter and the Reich-Legate that I expect no more from them than the usual courtesies afforded to a head of State. Our relationship is not a personal one you understand, but has more the character of a figurative association, not between personalities but between entities, even one may say between abstractions. Do you follow me, Reich-Minister?'

For once in his life Goebbels was at a loss. His foxy face looked blank. He found no words, so Parry-Morris proceeded.

'I rather think, although I can hardly believe my ears, that I heard you inquire if I had no respect for the Führer. I must tell you now, Reich-Minister, that my respect for Herr Hitler is similarly of a theoretical or even hypothetical nature. I believe my compatriot Lloyd George (whose commitment to the Welsh cause, I regret to have to tell you, was less than absolute, but who was of course a great statesman on the world stage) – I believe Mr Lloyd George expressed a somewhat analagous view when he returned from his meeting with Herr Hitler before the war. It was not, he said confidentially upon his return to this country, a meeting of minds, but a meeting of hypotheticals. I dare say Herr Hitler felt rather the same. Perhaps he has spoken to you of the occasion, Dr Goebbels?'

'Yes, yes,' said Goebbels as though hypnotized. 'Several times he has spoken to me of it.'

'Ah yes, I thought it possible. It is often said that the effect of the Welsh personality upon strangers cannot easily be expunged. But as you so perceptively remarked a few moments ago, Reich-Minister, we neither of us have illusions with respect to our present circumstances. We know where we stand, do we not. You need have no fears on that account. The matter of the language is not, of course, one that will impede the way of progress for our Homeland: and if I may say so, it is an honour to receive you here, Dr Goebbels, here in the Parliament House of my great predecessor Owain Glyndŵr – on behalf not only of our resurgent Welsh nation, but no less on behalf of all the generations of Welsh patriots who have, down the centuries, fought so consistently for their national, cultural and linguistic rights.

'And now, Herr Reich-Minister, I hear our guests returning from their tour, as enlightened, I hope, as they have been entertained. Shall we join them for refreshments?'

5 *Another saying in Welsh*

As in a daze, Goebbels allowed himself to be shown to the door. 'I think you must be mad, Parry-Morris,' was all he could say. 'Perfectly mad.'

'We have another saying in Welsh: "The madman knows not how mad he is".' And as the Gauleiter, Schinkel and the officials of the Propaganda Ministry rose somewhat anxiously to greet Dr Goebbels in the ante-room, the Llyw gently closed the door behind him.

DECISION

1 *A great success*

On the face of things the visit of the neutrals was a great success.The Propaganda Ministry distributed, of course, many scores of happy pictures, showing smiling Welsh people greeting their visitors with songs, flowers and recitations, showing Goebbels surrounded by grateful citizens of the Homeland and wearing a large daffodil in his buttonhole, showing visitors from the United States, Japan, Switzerland, Ireland, Portugal, Sweden and the International Red Cross inspecting factory floors and being fed on traditional Welsh oatcakes, above all showing Y Llyw shaking hands with Goebbels and posing with the Reich-Minister, the Gauleiter and the Legate beneath a large red dragon flag.

Everyone was delighted with the results. Many a feature article described the Homeland as evidence of Germany's true desire for a new Europe in which all its peoples, under the sheltering patronage of the Reich, would be free to honour their own identities. Even some of the most liberal and cynical American commentators were won over, and in London Lord Blankenthorpe, asked in the House of Lords for his comments, said he was most happy to pay tribute to this achievement of the protecting Power, which as it happened fulfilled one of the profoundest aspirations of the Associate Government, namely to bring proper fulfilment to all those ancient nations and proud peoples who constituted the United Kingdom.

2 *However*

However a different picture was presented by Dr Goebbels to the Führer, when he dropped in at the Chancellory for tea on his return to Germania. Cymru Newydd was a madhouse, he said. The whole thing was a farce, and a risky farce. Only the long-practised skills of his information officers had saved the entire visit from being a propaganda disaster. The meagre rations and long working hours of the people were beginning to show, in haggard faces and wasted frames (and was showing too, Goebbels strongly suspected, in lowered production levels – whatever Schinkel claimed). It had been extremely difficult to drum up the necessary festive spirit of welcome, and they had been obliged to hide half the population away, to conceal both their ill-health and their obvious resentments. As it was, undesirable contacts had almost certainly been made between visitors and inmates – he himself had overheard one of the tea-serving women making all-but-treasonable comments to an American.

'I have an uncomfortable feeling about them, Adolf, an uncomfortable feeling, not unlike the feeling I used sometimes to have – do you remember? – when the Jews were still around to plague us. And most unsettling of all, *mein Führer*, is that crazy man Parry-Morris.'

'Crazy? Is he crazy? How is he crazy? I'm going to accept a medal from him.'

'Crazy in what I assume to be a Welsh way. He quoted to me some incomprehensible saying about the Welsh attitude to madness, to the effect that madmen don't know when they are mad. My own feeling is that mad is mad, and that Parry-Morris is a lunatic.'

'What's the problem, then? We will eliminate him. He's got to go some time.'

'True, true, thank God. But there are difficulties.'

'Aha, but we have our proverbs too,' said Hitler, neatly plopping a lump of sugar into his tea. 'Do you know the old Bavarian one, Goebbels, about manure stinking more the longer you leave it lying about? No difficulty is too great, Goebbels, for the great sanitary operation that is the Third Reich. No heap of cow-manure can block our path. We are the scourers of dung, we are the cleansers, we are the de-lousers and the rat-catchers! Have we not,' said he, delicately choosing a cucumber sandwich, 'already scrubbed Europe clean of three, four, five million Jews?'

'Indeed we have, but Parry-Morris does pose problems of a rather different kind from those presented by that other Chosen Race. For one thing the whole construction of our propaganda exercise concerning Wales, which has so far proved such a success, especially in America, is built upon his inspiring presence.'

'He is inspiring? How inspiring?'

'No of course he isn't. He's an old fool. I was using what is called irony.'

'I see. Get rid of him then.'

'Well yes, we will of of course in the end, but unfortunately he has acquired such a propaganda image. The Americans think he is a marvellously benevolent representative of – well, of yourself, *mein Führer*, in a way . . .'

And finding that all the cucumber sandwiches had gone, Goebbels turned to a chocolate torte instead.

3 *The way Adolf Hitler's mind was directed*

'Bugger the Americans. Here is my decision. I am a decisive man, Josef, you know that. I live by decisions. It was always said of me, even when I was a boy, that I made up my mind in an instant, and never wavered in my determinations. So it is today. Here are my decisions concerning Wales. First, your crazy friend Parry-Morris must be removed, but not before he is brought to Germania to give me my medal. Secondly, the enterprise must now be wound down towards its final solution. The Lost Tribes have served their propaganda purposes: let the world now forget them – those American morons soon lose interest. You understand these decisions, Goebbels? You understand the way my mind is directed?'

'Perfectly, *mein Führer*. But that madman's medal? You really still intend to accept the medal?'

'Oh yes Goebbels, let's go ahead with the medal. What a joke it will be! The Order of the Dragon, what? Or the Harp, isn't it? Or the mistletoe – wasn't that a Druid thing? What a laugh! Don't tell Himmler – he believes in all that crap, you know – just get the man over here one day next week, right? A Last Outing for the Last Leader.'

'I will take the necessary steps. And now perhaps we may turn to a more attractive subject. I have been consulting with dear Fraulein Riefenstahl, and we believe the time has come for an anniversary rally at the Olympic Stadium. The event will culminate in a fly-past of a thousand of the Lancaster bombers we captured from the RAF, each one flying a Swastika from its bomb-bay . . .'

'Lovely idea,' said the Führer.

INVESTITURE

1 *Parry-Morris goes to Germania*

So Parry-Morris, in response to the Führer's summons, went to to Germania. He went in some style, too, accompanied by Heinrich Schinkel. Seen off by a somewhat raggle-taggle honour guard from his own *Plant Owain*, early one morning he was driven in the Legation Mercedes to the military airfield at Oswestry and flown to Germany in a Junkers belonging to the Foreign Ministry. At Tempelhof airport, in the heart of the capital of Europe, he was met by functionaries from the Chancellory and a posse of cameramen. As he left the aircraft the Llyw posed for his photograph graciously, as to the manner born, and had a kindly word in Welsh with the aircraft crew, who did not understand a word of it, but who responded respectfully. It was to be a day trip only – lunch with the Führer at the Chancellory, back to the Homeland in the evening – and it was described afterwards, by Goebbels to his wife, as a meeting of lunacies.

Hitler did not rise, did not indeed look up, when, at the end of the famous Long Walk of intimidation through the Chancellory ante-rooms, the Llyw arrived before the Führer's desk, Schinkel in attendance. The room was silent. Goebbels sat at Hitler's side, examining a document with him. Two rigid sentries stood behind the desk, and two uniformed functionaries bent carefully over Hitler's shoulder, ready to replace pages or offer supplementary files. Nobody spoke.

Parry-Morris was not discountenanced, though. Choosing a chair for himself he sat down, crossed his legs and placed his old-fashioned black bag beside him on the floor.

After an appalled moment or two Schinkel clicked his heels and barked a *Heil Hitler*. Goebbels coughed gently. Hitler looked up, took in the situation and burst into laughter. 'You must be the mad Welshman,' he said. 'I've been expecting you. Who but a madman behaves like this in the presence of the leader of all Europe? What, Schinkel, is he always like this? What is he up to? What are you playing at, you, Welshman? Are you playing games with me? Oh, a very good joke, a very good joke, a killing joke don't you think Goebbels?'

Parry-Morris, as usual, took a deep breath before replying. 'It is perfectly true, mein Führer,' he said, 'that in days long ago, when Wales was, under the sovereignty of its own native princes, an independent congeries of native principalities, celebrated by some of the great European poets of the day, including the divine Dafydd ap Gwilym, with whose work your Excellency is doubtless familiar –'

'Never heard of him", interjected the Führer.

'– it is perfectly true that in those halcyon days of our heritage our people, despite social circumstances which were by no means ideal – and were in some ways, one has to admit, inferior to those obtaining in many other countries of Europe, though not perhaps in the Celtic regions – despite these disadvantages, as I say, our people were well-known for their merriment, jollity and wit.

'This temperamental trait was inevitably subdued down the generations by the unhappy circumstances of English oppression – from which, I may say, your own generous and enlightened policy is at last releasing us – but still we like to think that at our best we retain some talent for entertainment. I would not wish you to suppose, however, your Excellency, that my manners have been disrespectful: in selecting for myself a chair, during your moment of profound preoccupation just now – and believe me, Your Excellency, I know full well how the weight of great responsibility can remove one in thought and intention from the present environment – I was merely exerting the prerorogative of one Head of State in meeting another.'

'You're right, Goebbels, the man's off his head,' was Hitler's response. 'Do you not realize, Parry-Morris, that by a click of my fingers I can have you sent off to Upper Silesia, if you know where that is?'

The Llyw did not seem to hear. 'Indeed, Your Excellency, I was about to exert another prerogative of my position as our own Leader – our own Führer, one might say – to invite you to become the very first recipient of the new honour which I have recently instituted for our small republic, membership of the Order of Llywelyn and Glyndŵr.' So saying, he dived into his Gladstone bag and produced a large plain medal of beaten iron, engraved with highly speculative images, side by side, of the two Welsh heroes.

'But before I present it, Your Excellency, may I say – you are familiar with the histories and significances

86

of these two national champions of ours? Should I explain their historical meaning for our reborn nation?'

'No, no,' said Hitler, laughing, 'for God's sake get on with it, Parry-Morris, I haven't got all day,' and so saying, to the astonishment of the bystanders, he bowed his head and allowed the Llyw to place over it the plain green ribbon of the order – declaiming in a loud voice, as he did so, an elaborate citation in Welsh. Hitler was vastly amused. 'Well done Parry-Morris, you lunatic,' he cried, 'said like a man' – and Goebbels, Schinkel and everyone else applauded, laughed loudly and were wreathed in smiles. 'You remind me very much, Parry-Morris,' said Hitler, 'of your compatriot Lloyd George. I always thought I could have done business with that man, if he had been in power. And I feel I have done good business with you – isn't that so, Goebbels?' And as he rose from his desk he laughed immoderately and placed his somewhat stubby finger down the side of his nose. 'And now, *Excellency*, after the great honour you have done me, let's go and eat.'

2 *The three pillars of history*

Hitler really was rather taken with Parry-Morris. For the first time in many years his luncheon table was not dominated by his own conversation, but by the booming monologues of the Llyw, and after lunch Hitler took him off in his big black armoured limousine – 'just the two of us, the Master of Europe and the Master of Wales' – for a tour of the new Berlin – 'our Germania, the capital and High Place of our new Europe, to which your own infinitesimal country, Parry-Morris, owes its allegiance and its loyalty.'

Up one great new boulevard they went, and down another, and through the vast Palace of the People with its massed names of the war dead. 'Terrible, what, Parry-Morris? Terrible but beautiful. So many splendid lives given to the Fatherland and to the new Europe. Can you not see their strong brown young torsos in the sun, or in the snows, singing and fighting and looking towards the dawn – and behind them our young German maidens, flaxen and strong too, always ready to support their menfolk? Speak, Parry-Morris. Say something.'

'It is hard for me to comment, Your Excellency. You must understand that your civilization and mine, though indeed they may have common roots in the distant past, as your adoption of the Sanskrit symbol of the Swastika may seem to testify – our cultures have diverged so widely in the intervening centuries that our values and traditions are by now somewhat alien to each other.'

'Alien? what do you mean, alien?'

'Oh, not alien in any essential sense. No race is altogether alien to another – it was a poet of Welsh descent, you know, who taught us that no man is an island – but alien in that we have come to attach different interpretations upon historical progressions.'

'What rubbish you do spout, Parry-Morris. A race is a race, is it not, an Aryan is an Aryan, a Slav is a Slav, a Jew is a Jew – or was. We all know that. History is confirming that before our eyes. Why, in your own case, the case of you Welsh, destiny is working itself out just as we foresaw – for we seize destiny, Parry-Morris, we Germans, you must understand that, destiny is our slave. What the future holds in store for you and your people is in the hands of destiny, but a destiny channelled and directed by the energies of the Master-Race. You do understand that, Parry-Morris? It is a matter of race, destiny and mastery – the three pillars of history. Race, destiny and mastery,' and Hitler slapped one hand upon his own knee, there in the back of the limousine, and put the other almost tenderly upon the Llyw's shoulder.

'Just as you say, Führer,' Parry-Morris replied.

3 *Scum, of course*

When they reached Templehof, where Goebbels and Schinkel were waiting for them, the Führer himself saw Parry-Morris to his waiting Junker , and watched it trundle down the runway flying its twin flags, Swastika and Red Dragon, until they were withdrawn into the

89

cockpit just before take-off. Parry-Morris did not return the Führer's salute, merely waving in a rather off-hand way, but even this did not seem to antagonize the Master of Europe.

'Scum of course,' he said to Goebbels as they stood side by side at the VIP urinals before returning to the Chancellory, 'anybody can see he's neo-Hebrew shit, but he amuses me.'

'Could it possibly be,' returned Goebbels, 'that you amuse him too?'

At that Hitler's face darkened rather, and he did up his fly-buttons meditatively. 'Get rid of him anyway,' he said, 'and all the cursed rest of them.'

CONFRONTATION

1 *Retirement Order*

When Y Llyw returned to his kingdom he found that word of the Führer's decision had preceded him. A Retirement Order had been drafted by the Protecting Power, and a copy awaited him in his office – in Welsh and in German too, as Parry-Morris found to his horror:

> *All citizens of Cymru aged 65 and over are to prepare themselves for transfer to the Honour Home in Eryri, together with citizens holding certificates of unfitness for productive work. Citizens will be informed when to report for transport, but are to hold themselves ready for movement at any time.*
>
> *By Order Y Llyw*

2 *Parry-Morris on his high horse*

'And what is the meaning of this?,' the Llyw demanded of Schinkel. By whose authority was this proclamation drafted? By what right is my name appended to it? What is the state of preparation of the Honour Home, and why have I not been given the opportunity of inspecting it? This is a disgraceful betrayal of all that has been promised me by the Reich authority. The Führer himself, I am sure, with his declared interest in the future and welfare of the Welsh people, would be horrified to hear of this atrociously high-handed treatment of a national leader from whose hands, only yesterday, he was pleased to receive the highest honour that our nation can bestow. By what right is this done, Schinkel? I demand to know. I demand the right to seek the intercession of the Führer himself. I speak not as a private individual, but as the Head of State of a constituent nation within the New Order of Europe.'

'Calm down, Llyw,' said Schinkel, 'and face the facts, unhappy though they may be. The New Order of Europe is the order of Nazi Germany, and you have no more rights in it than anybody else conquered by force of German arms and now absolutely at the command of German authority. The Führer himself will send Welsh people just wherever he likes whenever he likes, without consulting your so-called sovereignty, and if you haven't already realized that unfortunate truth you must be an ever greater booby than I took you for.'

Parry-Morris was apparently unmoved by this outburst. 'Sit down, Legate,' he said courteously, seating himself at his Eisteddfod chair behind his desk. 'I am sure you do not mean what you are saying. You are carried away by the tension of the moment – a kind of lapse of manners and judgement to which all of us in positions of authority, by the nature of our demanding positions, are occasionally subject. It is the weight and pressure of our responsibilities that causes it: I noticed that even the Führer, in the course of our amiable conversation yesterday, permitted himself a few vulgarities which, I am sure, upon reflection he has regretted. Even I have occasionally found myself reverting to idioms, in the Welsh language naturally, which in the course of everyday intercourse I would certainly hesitate to employ.

'Now consider this, Schinkel. I am of the opinion that these persons will be removed to Eryri in order to exterminate them? Am I right? Do you deny it?'

Schinkel did not reply, so the Llyw continued.

'Very well. And I, by virtue of the authority invested in me by the Protecting Power as Head of the Welsh State, here and now refuse to allow this to happen.'

So saying, with a flourish he ripped the Retirement Order into small pieces, dropping it with a flourish into the waste-paper basket.

'Dear God in heaven, Parry-Morris,' Schinkel began, 'don't you realize . . .?'

'That by a click of the Führer's fingers I can be removed for ever to Upper Silesia, wherever that is? Certainly I do, Schinkel. But I am aware too that thanks to the attentions of your own Reich-Ministry I have achieved a certain status in the world at large. I am the one living symbol of your good intentions towards the peoples of Europe. I am the living representation of my people's honour – and of your own. You were so good as to show me the press cuttings from America, Sweden, Switzerland, Ireland, Portugal, Japan, heaven knows where, which resulted from the visit of the neutrals last month, and I know what dismay would be felt around the world if it became known that Cymru Newydd was nothing but a cruel hoax. We are not Jews hidden away in the depths of eastern Europe, you know. We are only a couple of hundred miles from London, where the neutral Press – and especially the Americans, who number many people of Welsh origin and sympathy among their men and women of influence – maintain, as far as they can, a vigilant scrutiny upon what happens in these islands. And to adopt your own vivid words, you must think me an even bigger booby than I am if you suppose I have not realized all this. So, Herr Legate, I expressly forbid the removal of these citizens to Eryri, and I demand the instant rescission of this proclamation, Please let me have written confirmation by tomorrow morning.'

3 Goebbels is unsure

'Ha, ha, ha!' chortled Adolf Hitler, when a very Bowdlerized version of this conversation reached him that same evening. 'That crazy Celtic bastard is a treasure. Is he off his head or what? He has gone too far now. Call his impertinent bluff at once. Tell Schinkel from me to get the transports moving, and put Parry-Morris on one of the first.'

But Goebbels was not so sure. Was it all bluff? So far the treatment of the Welsh had not been at all bad, their sovereignty had been formally respected, and there really had been little to be hidden from the Americans. *Gott in Himmel*, there had even been *concessions* on language! But as Parry-Morris had said, the first whispers that Cymru Newydd was not what it seemed, the first relegation of the Llyw to his true condition of clowning impotence, and things might be different. There were already voices in America urging a war of liberation against Nazi Europe. What would the response be if Cymru Newydd turned out to be a fraud? It was a miracle that the Germans were getting away with making Europe *Juden-frie*. Could they afford to risk all for the sake of exterminating a few hundred thousand miserable Celts?

4 *But Hitler makes up his mind in an instant*

'You are getting old, Goebbels!,' Hitler said. 'We are an Empire of 300 million. We are the conquerors of the earth. We can do what we like. Fuck the Americans. We have played with Parry-Morris too long. I am tired of him. He no longer amuses me. Get rid of him. I tell you what, wipe him off the face of his miserable little country on their national day. When is that, Goebbels? Look it up in that book of yours. All the countries of my Empire have their national days, for exterminating their leaders on – eh, Goebbels? For exterminating the scum on. For wiping them out of human memory. When? March 1st? Aha, oho! March 1! Of course, I remember now – one of my foretold days of destiny. How infallible is Fate! And which particular decadent so-called saint is remembered on that day? St David? Well then, tell the *Reich-Kontrolle* people to see to it that on St David's Day the so-called Llyw is to say goodbye to his people.'

CONSPIRACY

1 *Dinner at the Reich-Legation*

But it was only September, and for the time being the Retirement Order was suspended. Cymru Newydd proceeded on its increasingly dingy way – rations getting shorter, work getting harder, patriotic exhortations less convincing. There were no further Press days, but a still frequent visitor from London was Lord Brackenthorpe, who made a monthly inspection visit with Gauleiter von Harden. Von Harden enjoyed his company. 'A splendid fellow. A real gentleman. When they say you can trust the word of an Englishman, they were thinking of men like him – Aryan through and through, sharing our principles and purposes, just the kind of Englishman the Führer can do business with.'

Parry-Morris, on the other hand, treated the Associate Government Minister with distaste. When they both dined with the Gauleiter at the Reich-Legation he sat there uncharactistically silent, replying to Brackenthorpe's sallies with frigid smiles, and seldom even referring to the glories of Welsh poesy and tradition. Even the Llyw, it seemed, was inhibited by Brackenthorpe's well-bred powers of Parliamentary sarcasm and wit. One night however something unexpected happened. They had ended dinner as usual with some of the Legate's excellent Madeira. 'How fortunate,' von Harden said, 'that our Portuguese friends, though as yet unconvinced of the advances of our united Europe, should still be willing to supply the Reich with their excellent dessert wines!'

'There's nothing like a panzer division on one's frontier,' observed Brackenthorpe, 'to ensure a flow of favours.'

'You may not realize,' Parry-Morris said, 'that in medieval times we in Wales produced wines known throughout Europe. Indeed the well-known bard –'

But Brackenthorpe interrupted him. 'If what we hear is true, when it came to strong drink your well-known bards knew what they were talking about.'

Parry-Morris was silenced, but when the dinner broke up, and they rose from the table, he was surprised to find Lord Brackenthorpe take him by the arm. 'Come Llyw,' he said, 'we must not be at each other's throats. We are both beneficiaries of the Reich, are we not – isn't that right, Gauleiter? Surely we can regard each other as political allies, if not personal friends. The Associate Government, as you must know, wishes Cymru Newydd every success in the future. Come, take a turn with me around the Reich-Legate's charming garden, before we go to bed – you'll excuse us, Schinkel, won't you?'

'Of course, of course,' said the Legate: and when the Minister and the Llyw had left the room the Gauleiter turned to him and said: 'You see, Schinkel? Have I not often told you how subtle and sensitive is English diplomacy? Lord Brackenthorpe is to Parry-Morris as a thoroughbred is to a cart-horse, and has no more faith in the future of Cymru Newydd than we have ourselves, yet his attitude to Parry-Morris, so calm, so serene, yes, so *gentlemanly* – that is something that all of us, Schinkel, even those of us within the Party hierarchy, might well try to emulate.'

2 *A stroll in the gardens*

Out in the moonlit garden the Welshman and the Englishman strolled round and round the flowerbeds (lovingly tended by a former head gardener from Bodnant, the greatest of Welsh gardens). For a time they walked in silence, the Minister, his hands negligently in his pockets, towering head and shoulders above the Llyw.

'I've been wanting to have a little talk with you, Llywelyn,' said Brackenthorpe. 'I may call you Llywelyn, may I?'

'You may not,' Parry-Morris instantly retorted, 'you are in Cymru now, and accustomed though you may have been in the old British-dominated Wales to patronize or ignore us, poor and impotent though we may still be, at least we now have the right to be addressed with the courtesy an ancient comity deserves.'

'Oh my dear fellow.' Brackenthorpe responded, 'forgive me. You are quite right, of course. Nevertheless, although I myself am more generally known as Edward, Lord Brackenthorpe of Brackenthorpe in the County of Sussex, you may if you wish address me as Iorwerth.'

Iorwerth! Parry-Morris stopped dead in his tracks.

He was not easily surprised, but he was taken aback. Iorwerth – the Welsh equivalent of Edward! 'You need not play with me, Lord Brackenthorpe,' he said. 'You need not make fun of our aspirations. If it were not for our nation's devotion, down the centuries, to our beloved language and all its forms, there would be nobody speaking Welsh today, and certainly no Cymru Newydd, however illusory and even ridiculous it may seem to you.'

'Ah but that's just it,' said Brackenthorpe. 'That's just what I wanted to talk to you about, away from the Gauleiter's ears. Was it not said, Llywelyn, that most peoples' truths are like straight lines, but that the Welshman's truth is more in the nature of a curve? Well, my friend, there is something a little curvy to my own conception of integrity, and that is perhaps because I am half-Welsh myself.

'You don't believe me? Well, I can't blame you, but I assure you that my grandmother was an Evans from Tregaron – Welsh-speaking, a very Welsh lady, as suspicious as you are yourself of everything English. When I was a child she called me Iorwerth always, and fed me a diet of Welsh fairy tales, even a smattering of your Welsh poetry.'

Parry-Morris walked on in silence. The situation seemed to be reversed, and it was Brackenthorpe who was now uncertain, almost a supplicant.

'You do believe me, Parry-Morris, don't you? Look, look. I brought this to prove it to you' – and from his wallet he pulled out an old brown photograph, and showed it to Parry-Morris in the moonlight. It showed two small children, eight or nine years old, posed side-by-side on a sofa, one dressed in a cloth cap and speckled scarf, the other in the tall-crowned hat of the traditional Welshwoman. 'You see, Llywelyn Bach,' he said rather self-consciously, 'there we are, my sister Rose and I, posed for our pictures at the photographers in Tregaron, before the chapel fancy dress party. We were going as clog dancers. On the left the Right Honourable the Lord Brackenthorpe, on the right Lady Paxton-Marshall, widow of the late Privy Seal. There you see the truth about me – I may not be full-blood Cymry like yourself, but in my veins there does truly run the blood of –'

'– the blood of the Llywelyns and Glyndŵr and Dafydd ap Gwilym and Howel Harris and Gwynfor Evans and – oh, my dear Brackenthorpe, my dear Iorwerth, forgive me my attitude. I had no inkling. I was blinded by circumstance. You have astonished me!

But now dear comrade' (and putting his arm in the Minister's, he led him once more around the bottom rhododendron grove), 'now you have told me this glorious truth, what can you do, in your position of privilege, to help the progress and the emancipation of our country?'

3 *'More than you think'*

Instantly Lord Brackenthorpe was once more a Minister of the Associate Government. 'I can do more than you think, Parry-Morris. I understand you, you know. Blood knows blood. But I know too that you cannot win this absurd battle of yours. Magnificent it may be, but it is not war. Listen to me now. We must not talk too long, von Harden will be wondering what we are up to. Listen to me. There may be a way in which I can help Cymru Newydd, and Cymru Newydd can help the world at large.'

'The world at large? My goodness.'

'We in the Associate Government are not all as abject as we look. We play along as well as we can, like you do. We act our parts. But – without telling you too many secrets – we have not altogether withdrawn from the real world. We have our contacts still in the free countries – in America, in Russia, in Canada. We are in sporadic touch with Churchill in Ottawa. Don't ask me how we keep open these lines of communication – just believe me that we do.

'Now as you must know, from the start of this war the chief British purpose was to draw the Yanks into the conflict on our side. With them we were bound to win it. Without them we were almost sure to lose. When Hitler went to war with the Russians, Churchill failed to persuade them that a Communist power could ever be an acceptable ally: and so it was that we were obliged to make our separate peace, and leave the Russians and the Germans to fight it out ever since. You are with me, Parry-Morris?'

'Perfectly, Iorwerth.'

'It remains our purpose still, despite everything, to persuade public opinion in America that it is their national duty to get rid of this monstrous Reich – to open (to coin a phrase) a Second Front and oblige the Germans to fight both in the east and the west. Without a doubt they would win the war for us.'

'And Cymru Newydd? How does our small country enter this portentous equation?'

Brackenthorpe was silent for a moment. 'You do know, Llywelyn, don't you, that the Nazis have no love for the Welsh? I'm told that Hitler himself has a fanatical dislike of you, I don't know why.'

'Such an ingrate,' sighed the Llyw. 'We have given him a medal, too.'

'Yes, well, you are expendable to him anyway. You know what is happening to the Jews? Sooner or later – sooner, I rather think – that will be the fate of the Cymry too, when your uses are finished. Did you realize that, Llywelyn? Tell me frankly – did you know that all along?'

'Our last home is already being prepared for us,' Parry-Morris simply said.

'Exactly. Spot on. But in the meantime you have

decided propaganda value for them. As you are well aware, they have convinced the world that Cymru Newydd, and you in person, are pledges of a decent German Reich. Complete and utter balls, but they've managed it. They're clever bastards, especially that Goebbels. So you mean a lot to them, Parry-Morris, however much they despise the lot of you. In their perverse way they're proud of you.'

'Yes. It has sometimes occurred to me, in the long hours of the night (my quarters are somewhat inadequately heated, despite the best efforts of my staff to gather firewood) – it has sometimes occurred to me that if perhaps emissaries could travel to the United States from the very midst of our community, from the belly of the cow as we say in Welsh, and were to reveal the truth about Cymru Newydd –'

'– from the horse's mouth.'

'If you prefer it . . . Had such a possibility occurred to your own minds?'

'Precisely such a possibility. Got it in one. Just what I wanted to have a word with you about. The thing is, you see, that if you could provide the right sort of messengers, we could more or less guarantee to get them there. But we need the right sort, Llywelyn. We need young, personable Welsh people, who can touch those Yankee hearts, none of your old windbags . . . Oh dear, excuse me Llwyelyn, I was not of course . . .'

'Of course not. It would never have occurred to me. No, no. But as it happens I do already have such a pair of representatives in mind.'

'You have? Llywelyn, you're a wonder. We'll get them there, believe you me; and once the Americans realize the truth about all this, by God, before you are exterminated you may find yourselves liberated!'

'Liberated in freedom!' Parry-Morris wildly shouted, before Brackenthorpe shushed him. 'Our destiny fulfilled! All our prophecies fulfilled! All our poetry justified! The sacrifice of the ages, everything our small nation has suffered under the iniquities of history, honourably redeemed at last!'

'Yes! and you yourself, dear friend, always to be remembered as the saviour of your country!'

'Proceed with the plan, Lord Brackenthorpe,' said the Llyw portentously. 'You have my authority.'

4 *English humour*

Schinkel and von Harden were still smoking their last cigars when Brackenthorpe returned to the Reich-Legation, having dropped off Parry-Morris at his own quarters with fervent handshakes and rather a long Welsh benediction. 'Well, well, Brackenthorpe,' von Harden said fron his armchair beside the fire, 'you *have* had a long conversation with our Last Leader. How did it go?'

'Give me a whiskey, Schinkel, there's a good fellow. How that man does talk! Jabber, jabber, poetic destiny and all that. You must have the patience of Job – oh, forgive me Gauleiter, not Job, that would never do – the patience of Parsifal, shall we say? Was Parsifal patient? Who was Parsifal?'

'Oh Brackenthorpe, you and your English humour.

You will have me sent to a camp in the end – unless you're sent there yourself first!'

And so the three men laughed and drank and smoked, until the time came for bed. 'Heil Hitler,' said von Harden to Schinkel. 'Heil Hitler,' said Schinkel to von Harden. 'Nighty-night,' said Brackenthorpe to both of them, 'mind the bugs don't bite' – and how they laughed as they parted!

Across the road Parry-Morris, by the light of his hurricane lamp, was busy into the small hours writing a *cywydd* on the Curvatures of Truth.

INTERVENTION

1 *Two emissaries went*

At first nothing much happened. Life in Cymru Newydd continued uneventfully, marked only by a perceptible decline in almost everything. The buildings, never very spanking, grew shabbier. The factories worked slower. The citizens themselves, their clothes now patched and threadbare, began to acquire the grey testy look of people who are certainly not on the edge of famine, but whose appetite is never quite satisfied. The Reich-Legation, with its beautifully-kept gardens of hydrangeas and rhododendrons, began to look cruelly anomalous. 'It's starting to show,' said Sir Gwilym Adam-Jones, drinking ersatz coffee with Miriam and Angharad. 'The claws,' as the poet said, 'beneath the velvet'.'

'What poet was that, dear?' said Miriam spikily.

'Who he was momentarily escapes me. What he said is all that matters. And it confirms what I – what we – have been saying all along. That Parry-Morris, if he's not a mere scoundrelly collaborator, is a miserable dupe. I can't understand the man. One day he's quite bravely standing up to them, the next he's walking around the Embassy garden actually arm in arm with the despicable Brackenthorpe. And have you noticed how often he dines with Schinkel these days? How does all that fit in with his long-vaunted patriotism?

Cymru Rhydd indeed – Cymru Free! Cymru betrayed would be more like it, and made to be a mere propaganda tool of the Third Reich.'

Miriam could not understand the Llyw either, and said so in language less temperate: but Angharad remained silent, and a week or two later, with her friend Emrys, she disappeared from Cymru Newydd.

2 *Reluctance to deceive the Protecting Power*

'Dear me,' said the Llyw when, sitting at his Presidential desk beside the red dragon flag on its oak flagstaff (presented by the Foreign Press Association of London after the visit of the neutrals), he was given this news by his Chief Clerk, Chef-de-Protocol and Chief of Administration.

'Dear me, a blow for you, Master' – for he still observed the old college courtesies towards Sir Gwilym – 'and a decided setback of course for Cymru Newydd, even though the disappearance of these young persons is undoubtedly no more than a lovers' escapade. They will doubtless soon be apprehended, but reluctant as I am to deceive the Protecting Power, I fear that the news of their elopement must be kept to ourselves for as long as possible. I will undertake myself to smooth matters over with Legate Schinkel.'

(Oh yes? thought Adam-Jones cynically to himself. I wonder how that will be?).

'It is the hierarchy at Oxford that we must protect ourselves against – and not least your poor daughter and her paramour. May I take it, Master, that you can arrange matters at the morning roll-call? Good. Then I will make sure nothing appears in the manifestos. Young Owen works in Unit 4, I believe? I will arrange a substitute. At all costs – you understand, Master? – we must not allow the Protectorate to suppose that Cymru Newydd is in any way disloyal to the Reich, even by an excess of young love. We must at all costs maintain the present satisfactory relationship, under which our beloved country is truly acquiring, as you may see as you look around you, the true attributes of a sovereign nation. Observe the Draig Goch beside me, Master, on its oaken flagstaff! That is the pledge of our independence, the ancient pledge of Llywelyn and Glyndŵr, handed to us down the generations, down the centuries, hallowed by the loyalty of a thousand saints and poets of our race. It is our great privilege, Master, to be its agents and its witnesses. We must make sure, Master, that we do not betray it now. You understand me, Gwilym?'

And so things were arranged.

3 *Bagpipes from the barracks*

Nevertheless the citizens of Cynmru Newydd were surprised to discover that they had some new guards. The rickety old Wermacht veterans disappeared from the barrack blocks outside the perimeter fences, and borne on the evening breezes the Welsh now heard a Scottish skirl of pipes. The Homeland was now guarded by the Bonnie Prince Charlie Division, whose kilted uniforms, with their Death's Head sporrans, soon became a familiar sight on the other side of the wire. The division had been posted there, Parry-Morris was told, at the specific order of the Führer.

'Be that as it may, I must officially protest,' the Llyw told the Reich-Legate. 'The arrival of these troops, and their stationing within perpetual sight of our independent citizenry, is a blatant provocation, and an affront to the sovereignty of Cymru Newydd.'

'I don't see that at all, Llyw,' Schinkel blandly replied. 'Within the imperial territories of the Reich we Germans have a perfect diplomatic, political and moral right to station troops wherever we please. It is indeed a courtesy on our part that we have confined these highly-disciplined soldiers to territory outside the frontiers of Cymru Newydd. And besides, Parry-Morris, is it not true that these gallant Scottish warriors are your fellow-Celts? I believe that was the Führer's whimsical thought, in having them sent here.'

4 *What happened to Angharad and Emrys?*

What had happened to Angharad and Emrys nobody learnt for weeks. *Cymru Ar Goll*, Cymru Lost, as Parry-Morris had dubbed the larger Wales beyond the Homeland, had undergone a thorough process of ethnic cleansing after the establishment of Cymru Newydd. The countryside was empty and desolate. The market towns had mostly been deliberately destroyed. The industrial cities and seaports had been repopulated with immigrants, some voluntary, some forced – Latvians, Ukranians, Czechs, Basques, a few English, together with cadres of German managers to run the coal mines and steel works and manage the ports. There were no Welsh people left to maintain contact with Cymru Newydd. Wales Lost was no longer Wales at all: by the deliberate policy of the Reich, which believed in small and easily controlled political units, it was no longer even British. 'There are no gentlemen in Wales,' von Hardin had told his administrators, 'you may do what you like with the place. As for the Welsh, the bloody Taffys as our friend Brackenthorpe calls them, they are taken care of already.'

But once again on one of his monthly visits, Brackenthorpe took Parry-Morris aside.

'So, Llyw, I hear strange rumours, what? I have heard it said in London that some of your people have, so to speak, declined the hospitality of Cymru Neywdd and absconded to the wider world.'

'I know nothing of it,' said Parry-Morris. 'If some of our citizens have decided to leave us, that is their business.'

'Of course you know nothing. Very wise too. But I have to warn you, Llywelyn, that it is only a matter of time before von Harden hears of it, and when he does you must make sure he thinks of it only as a personal adventure.'

'Relieve him of any misapprehension that these young persons may have some political or patriotic motive in mind, is that it? Relieve him of any suspicion that the Associate Government may be in some way cognizant of their intentions?'

'That's it exactly. Got it in one. You know as well as I do how much depends upon this – well, this adventure. It may well be that these two young people carry with them the future of Europe, the future of the world, and that it is to Wales, dear Wales, that mankind will owe its salvation.'

'Dear me, Iorwerth, you are beginning to sound a little like me.'

'Yes, sometimes my Welshness does get the better of me. But I am not the only crypto-Welshman in Downing Street now, you know. The PM himself claims some remote connection with Llandudno, and goes around the whole time quoting some old Welsh saw about cats and rent, new to me but you probably know it?'

'Milk for the cat, rent for the landlord'

'That's the one, I expect. Anyway the sweet old ditherer has warm feelings towards you – towards us – and it was not without his connivance that we contrived to get the young lovers out.'

'You've got them out? How have you done it?'

'Ah no, Llyw, we must have some secrets of our own. But I will tell you that the PM is Honorary Colonel of the Bonnie Prince Charlie Division, nominated to the job in a rash moment of romance by Hitler himself. Have you come across a Major Frazer-Mackintosh, over the wire there? No? Well, nuff said, eh? As to your young friends, you needn't worry about them. They are safely on their way – you'll see!'

5 *Proverb in German*

Sure enough, a few days later von Harden arrived in Machynlleth, and raised with Parry-Morris the subject of the missing couple. He was not unduly troubled by the news: he was sure they would soon be caught, and anyway he knew that the whole programme of Cymru Newydd was about to enter its last act. Still, he was rather gratified by the Llyw's abject apologies.

'It is a shame and a disgrace, Gauleiter, I admit it – as we say in Welsh, 'the horn of the ram dirties the fleece.' It is a betrayal of all we have tried to achieve in Cymru Newydd, and indeed of all that the Protecting Power has achieved on our behalf.'

'Don't distress yourself, Llyw. We have a proverb in German too, 'every kilo of apples has a rotten pear.' I am sure the Führer, when he is informed of this little mishap, will realize that it represents no lack of goodwill or of vigilance on your part. I am sure too that the miscreants will soon be apprehended and given their just deserts – Major Frazer-Mackintosh of the Bonnie Prince Charlies tells me that he has the entire countryside thoroughly covered, and of course if they ever venture over the frontier into England they haven't, as Lord Brackenthorpe would say, a hope in hell – an apt and colourful metaphor, don't you think Llyw, and very characteristic of the upper-class Englishman's versatile command of language.'

Parry-Morris did not reply, but he was satisfied with the exchange.

6 *An unexpected blow*

Faced with the Führer's implacable deadline, the Reich-Kontrolle proceeded diligently with the completion of the Honour Home. It was a loveless huddle of black huts, built in unyielding geometric lines in a narrow valley in the heart of Eryri, traditionally the last fastness of the Welsh princes. Nobody now lived in the neighbourhood. The old quarry village of Llanberis was deserted; the lines of the rack railway up Snowdon, the highest mountain in Wales, had been melted down for arms production. Next door to the camp were the barrack blocks of the SS-Kommando detailed to run the camp, when the time came. High electrified wires surrounded the Honour Home, with watch-towers, but the camp buildings looked flimsy and impermanent. They were not built to last. The most solid structures were the four gas chambers that stood at a little distance from the living huts, in the former churchyard of Llanberis church.

It was not a particularly large camp by recent standards – 'second-class facilities,' the SS men joked – but it came as a blow to their *amour propre*, and a nasty shock to the *Reich-Kontrolle*, and decidedly disturbing news to Gauleiter von Harden, and a revelation to the Llyw of Cymru Newydd, but not altogether a surprise to Lord Brackenthorpe and the old dodderer in Downing Street, when one autumn day six Mig precision bombers of the Soviet Navy suddenly screamed up the Llanberis valley and bombed the Honour Home to smithereens.

REVELATION

1 *They thought it was lemonade*

How Angharad and Emrys got out of Cymru Newydd, nobody quite knew, even themselves. Perhaps they were drugged? Somehow, anyway, they were smuggled by underground routes across Europe to Russia, where they arrived in a kind of daze and were handed over to the British Military Mission, still *en poste* in Moscow after so many years of exile. Early the very next morning they were taken into the presence of Marshal Vladimir Zuvotsky, victor of Novograd and now director of the Occupied Europe branch of the 15th Department.

Early though it was, Zuvotsky was already amiably drunk. He was charmed by his young Welsh visitors. He identified for them his multitudinous medals, one by one. He told them a lot about the Battle of Novgorod. He swore that his department would do anything to help the sacred cause of Wales, a country he had never heard of before. He seemed unsurprised to learn of the existence of the Honour Camp – 'I have been told of such places' – but promised to have it dealt with. 'For you, anything, my dears,' he burbled, pouring them all very large vodkas, 'we will soon get rid of it. Sh! Don't tell Comrade Stalin. Not a word! It will be our little secret.'

The meeting ended with toasts to Mother Russia and

Cymru Newydd, enthusiastically supported by Angharad and Emrys, who besides still being bleary from their journey had never tasted vodka before, and thought it was a sort of Russian lemonade.

2 *The task had not been easy*

Far away in Washington Emrys and Angharad had not yet been heard of, but the legend of Cymru Newydd had been extremely well propagated by the Germans. The British Information Service in Exile in the United States had gone through lean times for years, having hardly any money and very little to inform the Americans about, but had stuck manfully to its task, printing endless pamphlets ('Tally-ho! The Art and Style of English Fox-Hunting,' or 'How the Monarchy Works: Royalty in Modern Britain'), tirelessly lobbying newspaper editors, sending its meagre and ageing stock of lecturers to plead the British cause from coast to coast. Its one task was to bring America into the war, and it was not an easy one.

The Reich held all the cards. There was a huge and hospitable German Embassy in Washington, pro-German clubs and institutions abounded, bags of money was available and Dr Goebbels made sure that an endless flow of glamorous and persuasive show-biz personalities, writers, artists, athletes and academics crossed the Atlantic to represent the victorious new German Europe. When they had a tale to tell like the inspiring story of the Welsh Homeland, it received wide publicity everywhere. The poor British had little to offer in competition: until one autumn day there reached their ears the rumour that Cymru Newydd was not what it seemed – not the prime example of German tolerance and progressiveness that even they had half-accepted, but no more than a cheap deceit.

At last, something to propagate! Nobody had lately believed the constant rather monotonous British complaints about the state of things in occupied Europe – 'losers' talk,' newspapermen called it – but the stories about Cymru Newydd first surfaced in the reports of American reporters who had been there for themselves on the famous visit of the neutrals, and in retrospect had come to suspect something fraudulent: nothing firm, nothing sensational, but what the radio correspondent Ed Murrow called a 'suspicious smell' to it.

At first the public response had been muted. Wales seemed so insignificant a spot on the map of the new Europe. There was, however, a Welsh diaspora in the United States, and its lively newspaper, *Ninnau*, 'Ourselves,' naturally seized upon the rumours. Its editor demanded more information, more official enquiries by the American Embassy in Germania. One by one columnists across America picked up the story. Phone-in radio programmes began to talk about it. WHAT'S REALLY HAPPENED TO WALES? demanded the New York *Daily News*, in a big feature story, and TV pundits discussed the implications of the rumours 'in depth' (i.e. at great length). Foreign correspondents who had written glowingly about Cymru Newydd a year or two before now revealed that they had really shared the doubts of the great Murrow all along . . .

3 *Disadvantages of a Harvard education*

Then the Soviet Information Service put out a news statement:

> *On Thursday aircraft operating from the new Soviet aircraft carrier* Josef Stalin, *at the personal order of Marshal Stalin, bombed and destroyed the notorious extermination camp in so-called Cymru Newydd, on the west coast of Nazi-occupied England. The camp was eliminated, but thanks to the skill of our dedicated Soviet airmen and their advanced technical equipment no casualties were caused among the inmates, and all our aircraft returned safely. Reports say that many Fascist guards were killed.*

Coming after many months of drab communiques from the stagnant Eastern Front, this enigmatic announcement caused a sensation. Extermination Camp? Stalin's personal order? Inmates? What was this? At the President's weekly Press Conference many searching questions were asked, and answered diplomatically.

'Mr President, have you anything to tell us about the Soviet air raid on the so-called Welsh Homeland in England, and what its implications might be?'

'I have no information so far as to the truth of these implications. I have asked our Ambassadors in Moscow, Germania and London to make further inquiries.'

'Have our diplomats been to see this place for themselves? And if not, sir, why not?'

'Yes, Mrs Holman, I believe our diplomats have

117

been given an opportunity to visit the development, but I have no further information.'

'Can you tell us, Mr President, how to pronounce the name of the place?' (laughter)

'Alas Mr Alsop, my somewhat myopic parents gave me only the limited advantages of a Harvard education.'

4 *Celebrities!*

And then one morning there burst upon the scene Angharad and her Emrys!

They arrived at Washington military airport on one of the new Tupolev jets, which immediately returned to Russia for security reasons, and were whisked away to the British Embassy. 'We were expecting you,' said the Ambassador-in-Exile suavely. 'Marshal Stalin asked us to take care of you – what important young people you must be!'

Next day they were presented to the Press by the highly excited British Information Service, with promises to the assembled reporters of 'believe me, old boy, a really big story' ('Big my arse,' said one leathery hack to another, 'I know these British wimps . . .') But it was big, and Angharad and Emrys made headlines everywhere. They were the true stuff of propaganda. They were young and appealing. They looked pale, frail and nervous. They were clearly lovers. They talked with sad passion about their homeland, and told all they knew about the state of affairs in Cymru Newydd.

'You mean it's all a sham?'

'All a fraud, yes, just a front.'

'And what about this Parry-Morris, is he just a stooge for the Nazis?'

'Certainly not, he is a true patriot, he's a great Welshman, doing his best for his people.'

Inexperienced though they were, they never put a foot wrong.

'Miss Adam-Jones, what is the position of women in the society of Cymru Newydd?'

'We stand side by side with our menfolk in equality. We are all Welsh people.'

'What do they think of America in Wales these days?'

'They look upon your great country as their one hope of freedom, the last chance that truth will prevail. Because of you they can still hope that one day not just Cymru Newydd, but the whole of Europe can look forward to a happier future.'

'You mean we should go to war with Germany?'

'Our Llyw, Mr Parry-Morris, likes to quote an old Welsh proverb in answer to such questions. '*Defaid sy'n holi; y tarw sy'n ateb*' – it's the sheep that ask questions, the bull must answer them.'

5 *Sensation!*

They caused a sensation. Across America, week by week, a great swell of public opinion called for intervention in Europe. Welsh Americans, of course, were loudest in their demands, but they were joined by the powerful Jewish community, by French exiles and Italians, by dissident Germans. The administration found itself attacked from all sides for its naïvety and its timidity. What was really happening to the Jews of Europe? people were asking now. What about the Slavs, and the Gypsies? Could one believe anything the Nazis said? Huge charity organizations set up Welsh Relief Funds, and arranged food parcels for Cymru Newydd through the Red Cross. Angharad and Emrys became household names, figures of tragic romance and hope. They appeared on public platforms across the nation and were constantly on television, looking at each other soulfully in the eyes and appealing for intervention. As for Parry-Morris, he was elevated almost to sainthood – the Gandhi of Wales, the popular Press called him. Relations with the German Government collapsed. Embassies were withdrawn on both sides. The American correspondents left Reich-Europe, and the last of the sexy UFA stars, the splendid Olympic athletes, hastened home to the Fatherland. War seemed inevitable.

6 *The cat did appear to be among the birds*

In Moscow Captain Arseniev and Lieutenant Rudinsky went on television to explain their bombing mission.

'It was a perilous mission,' said the Captain, 'but we accomplished it for the sake of our oppressed Welsh comrades and for the glory of the Great Soviet Motherland. Fortunately we had excellent guidance from our superior officers and were supplied with the very best Soviet-made equipment. We were happy to be able to fulfil our instructions.'

And in Wales Parry-Morris smiled enigmatically at von Harden, down from Oxford yet again.

'Now then, Llyw,' said the Gauleiter. 'The cat appears to be among the birds. We have enjoyed a happy relationship in the past, I think you will agree –'

'Oh, absolutely, a happy and rewarding relationship.'

'– but the time has now come to hit the nitty-gritty. I am told the Führer himself is extremely disturbed by developments in America. Tell me, Parry-Morris, what do you propose should be done to rectify the damage and limit the danger caused by the irresponsible behaviour of these eloping fugitives?'

The Llyw smiled even more enigmatically. 'We have a proverb in Welsh,' he said, '*Defaid sy'n holi; y tarw sy'n ateb.*'

'Need I translate?' he added.

REPERCUSSIONS

1 *Yes, he had felt it in his bones*

They arrested Parry-Morris, but not very seriously. 'Shoot him,' Hitler had told Himmler. 'Tear him apart. I knew when he came here that he was a neo-Jewish bastard. He reminded me of that other Welsh swine – what was his name Goebbels? – yes, Lloyd George, that's the one, just the same decadent malicious conniving streak to him. My intuitions are never wrong. I feel things in my bones. I knew that Parry-Morris was a shit the moment I saw him. All his ridiculous prattle about poets and bards. That ridiculous bauble he put around my neck. Shoot him at once, Himmler, and get rid of his whole miserable rabble of Welsh Jews. I knew they were Bolsheviks all along. Get those ovens rebuilt and shove them all in. March 1st! Gas the lot of them by March 1st.'

But it was too late, and everyone but the Führer recognized it. 'WHERE IS PARRY-MORRIS?' the cry now screamed across the American headlnes, and even the Gauleiter began to hedge his bets. Having passed on the order to have the Llyw shot, he cautiously left the matter to the Reich-Legate, and the Llyw found himself merely confined in reasonable comfort to the Legation. 'Just you lie low,' said Schinkel, 'like the old fox you are, and we will see what happens.'

Everybody lay low, actually, watching the way the wind was blowing. Cymru Newydd was more isolated than ever not just from the rest of Europe, but even from the rest of Britain. With Parry-Morris out of action, the Master of Jesus acting as a bewildered Acting Llyw, and the people as a whole enervated by hunger and ignorance, one might expect the Welsh to be sadly demoralized, but it was not so. On the contrary. In one way and another news filtered through to them, often slipped through the wires by Scotsmen of the Bonnie Prince Charlies, and soon nobody was unaware that Emrys and Angharad had made it safely to Washington, and that there was an unmistakable public demand in the United States for the liberation of all Europe, and in particular of Wales. A new spirit of hope arose in the huts and cottages of Cymru Newydd.

The bandmaster for instance, athough by now he was almost too weak to raise a baton, was marvellously exuberant. 'Where there's the Welsh there's a way,' he used to cry – 'as our respected Llyw, God bless him, might have said, only in his impeccable Welsh of course.' Even Sir Gwilym was moved to claim that he had expected it all along. It had all been planned from the start, he explained.

2 *Pshaw, Miriam said, but . . .*

'Pshaw,' said Miriam; but be that as it may have been, very soon the vast American military machine was preparing for action. The US forces had been on full mobilization for years – ever since, in fact, the Nazi subjugation of Europe had been completed – and now they were placed on immediate red alert. 'Could you ever have doubted,' said the captive Llyw to his captor over breakfast at the Legation, 'that one day our Welsh example would have inspired the Great Republic to intervene on our behalf, and on behalf of all the oppressed nations of Europe? You perhaps do not realize, Schinkel, and it may surprise you to learn, the importance of Welsh influences in American affairs down the generations. For example more than fifty of the signatories of the Declaration of Independence were Welsh. Did you know that?'

'Nothing you tell me can surprise me, but more than fifty does seem a lot. I thought there were only 56 signatories in all.'

'The exact number is not important. Two out of the three first Presidents were undoubtedly Welshmen, and compelling recent evidence has lately been deduced to the effect that George Washington too had Welsh blood in his veins. Lincoln of course, as everyone knows, was descended from Rhodri Mawr the King of Gwynedd, and some scholars opine that his family name is itself no more than a corruption of Llyn Côn, meaning a conically-shaped lake. and probably a reference to the famous occasion when the dragon Medryn burst out of the drowned valley of Cwm Berwyn and flew away to the Court of Annwn. You remember that legend, Schinkel?'

'Not intimately, Llyw.'

'Never mind. As I was saying, who can doubt that with such profound historical and hereditary links with Wales, the Americans can long hold back from our liberation? I imagine they are preparing their forces even now.'

'Well they'd better hurry. I had a confirming execution order from Germania this morning, and any day now the Reich-Coroner will be arriving from Berlin to prepare an inquest for you.'

'Let him come! *Ut Omnes Veniant* – Let Them All Come! I care not whether I am dead or alive when our dear country regains its sovereign independence at last, and know that my spirit will be conjoined with those of our heroes of old, our bards *enwogion o fri*, in the annals of the Cymry for ever! You do remember, dear Schinkel, do you not, our conversation long ago concerning the symbolical relationship between past and present within the heritage of our people?'

'Oh I do, I do!' lied Schinkel. 'But how incorrigible you are, Llyw, what an irrepressible romantic! No wonder the Führer took to you.'

3 *I am He*

It happened very suddenly. After decades of war, and the incessant drain on morale and resources of the squalid fighting on the Russian front, the Germans made no attempt to resist attack from a new, fresh enemy 3,500 miles away across the Atlantic. Hitler forbade defensive preparations anyway.

'Those Jewish decadents,' he told his generals, 'they will never leave their whores and whiskies on Wall Street to fight us. Ignore them. Let them see our German contempt for them.' Even when the Americans broke off diplomatic relations – even when war was declared in a solemn Presidential speech on a February midnight – even when his intelligence chiefs repeatedly warned him of immediate American preparations for an assault, the Führer was adamant. 'Let them fart and belch as they like. They will never dare come. Take no notice.'

So it was that early one February morning an entire American airborne division, flown by the new long-distance Boeing transport jets, was dropped into Cymru Newydd – a symbolic announcement of the coming liberation of Europe. The very first the Welsh knew of it was some brief fighting along the perimeter wires, the Bonny Prince Charlies very soon abandoning resistance in the face of such overwhelming force. Soon after dawn that morning American paratroopers appeared in Machynlleth itself, cautiously advancing, at the crouch, through the hutments to the Reich-Legation.

Inside the house the Llyw and the Legate, sitting in the spacious and upholstered reception room, with its portrait of the Führer above the mantlepiece, self-consciously ignored the warlike noises outside – getting closer and closer to them, with shouts and banging of boots, and an occasional burst of automatic fire, until they were echoing along the corridors and up the stairs of the building.

'Not the Reich-Coroner, Schinkel, I rather think,' said Parry-Morris.

'Probably not,' said Schinkel. 'Congratulations'

And then the door burst open. Two hefty black paratroopers stormed in to stand guard on each side of the door, automatic rifles at the ready. One of them bawled: 'On your feet. Hands above your heads.

126

Lieutenant-General Lincoln J. Morgan, US Army, Commanding General of the Special Parry-Morris Airborne Division.'

Llyw and Legate rose to their feet, and into the room there strode a gigantic black general in steel helmet and dark glasses, revolver at his belt, sub-machine gun at his shoulder. 'Right then,' he shouted. 'Where is he? I'll give you ten seconds to answer' – and taking the gun from his shoulder he stood there patently ready to spray them with fire.

'Where's who?' said Schinkel.

'Where's who, you Nazi bastard? Where's who? Where's Llywelyn Parry-Morris, that's who, the Hero of Cymru Newydd, the Welsh Gandhi, that's who, the man my outfit's named for. What have you done with Parry-Morris?'

There was a chill silence. The General ostentatiously clicked his safety catch. The two bodyguards murmured something obscene. Then Parry-Morris diffidently stepped forward.

'STAY WHERE YOU ARE!' shouted the General and his soldiers in deafening unison, but the Llyw took no notice. Shuffling forward, he held out his hand to the enormous officer. 'I am He,' he said, and he gave it an unmistakable capital H. 'I am Llywelyn Dafydd Parry-Morris, Llyw of Cymru Newydd, Leader of the Welsh Republic. I am happy to welcome you to my country, especially with such credentials as your name guarantees – a Lincoln and a Morgan conjoined cannot but bring honour to your rank and family, just as your adoption of my own name for the title of your division brings honour to me, or more especially to my country.

127

Croeso gyfeillion, Croeso i Gymru – oh and by the way, General, this is my good friend and collaborator, and I may say a true friend to Cymru too, Heinrich Schinkel, by the turn of fortune's wheel at present the Reich-Legate in Cymru Newydd, but presently to be made an honorary citizen of the sovereign independent Republic of Cymru – Old, New and Eternal!'

The General stood there dumbstruck, extending his hand to be shaken as though in a dream. The bodyguards looked at each other and at their commander in bewilderment, while the Llyw, walking over to them, inspected them up and down and remarked 'Well done, gentlemen, very smartly turned out, and in very difficult circumstances – although I am a pacifist myself, thus following an old Methodist tradition in my family, I am not immune to appreciation of the military aesthetic.'

'YESSIR,' snapped the soldiers as one man: and as for Heinrich Schinkel, after a moment of astonished silence he burst out laughing, so loudly, so infectiously, so happily, that the General and the soldiers were presently laughing too, and even the Llyw allowed himself a dignified smile. 'Really, Llywelyn,' said the Reich-Legate, 'you really do take the biscuit, as your friend Lord Brackenthorpe would say.'

FULFILMENT

1 *Mr Churchill finds some apt phrases*

Before long Parry-Morris, General Morgan, Schinkel
and Major Frazer-Mackintosh were sitting with the
Adam-Joneses in the Legation drawing-room, drinking
some of Schinkel's last sweet Sauterne and listening to
the nightly BBC-in-Exile news from Ottawa. The
bulletin was interrupted to allow for a special broadcast
from Winston Churchill, Prime Minister-in-Exile of
Great Britain. None of them would ever forget his few
slurred words (he was very old indeed, and could not
speak in public for more than a few moments at a time).

'My fellow-citizens, wherever you are, we have all
heard with gratitude and rejoicing that the soldiers of
our gallant new ally, the United States of America,
have landed safely upon the shores of long-oppressed
Europe. Better, I might say to our friends in the
American Congress, better late than never!

'To quote one of the great American poets,
'Eastward, look, the land is bright!' And this new
radiance has fallen first upon a beloved member of our
own ancient family of nations: the honourable and
venerable nation of Wales, or Cimry, as I believe they
prefer to call it in that land of bards and heroes.

'Tonight then I can say to you all: Be of good heart!
I cannot yet declare these momentous events to be the
end of our long and terrible ordeal. They are perhaps

not even the beginning of the end. But perhaps I shall not be tempting Providence too far if I say that they are the end of the beginning. God Save The King!'

'He speaks truly,' pronounced the Llyw, 'questionable though his behaviour was in sending the troops to Tonypandy to suppress the miners' strike of 1926. We few, we happy few – as our great Welsh poet has it – are privileged to witness, from our different viewpoints, not simply the approaching conclusion of a tragic and titanic struggle, but also the birth of a nation. Let us drink to peace, to friendship, and to Cymru.'

'Peace, friendship, Cymru,' they all cried. Some had tears in their eyes, even Miriam but especially Schinkel, and it was Adam-Jones who broke the long and thoughtful silence that followed. 'All the same, Llyw, if I may venture to say so, it was hardly a Welsh poet who wrote those famous words.'

'In all the years I have known you, Master, in peace as in war, you have seldom seemed to know when to take me seriously.'

2 What became of Wales and the people of the fable

And so another Welsh fable found its own conclusion, and joined the folklore. Presently, in the fabulous way, it all came true. Out of the wreckage of Europe, when the war was won and Hitler was dead (he killed himself on St David's Day) there sprang as the Llyw had promised a new, brave, truly sovereign republic of Cymru, Wales, a respected member of the Confederation of Europe,

131

living in somewhat amused amity with its old enemy England next door. It was never rich, but it was happy. Its first President was, of course, Llywelyn Parry-Morris, old but indefatigable, and when it re-established its own Order of Llywelyn and Glyndŵr among those first distinguished were Lord Brackenthorpe and former Reich-Legate Schinkel. General Lincoln J. Morgan, US Army, was given the lifetime use of reconstructed chambers in Caernarfon Castle, in recognition of his services to the little State: he was greatly admired there, and was said to enjoy more than friendly relations with several ladies of the town. The ruins of the Welsh Honour Home were preserved as a national shrine; beside it was erected a memorial to the men of the Soviet Arctic Fleet which was shakily unveiled by Marshal Zuvotsky himself (in attendance, the former Cowley Works Band, now relocated in Wales, renamed the Liberation Ensemble and conducted for the occasion by its 95-year-old bandmaster emeritus).

Sir Gwilym and Lady Adam-Jones also preferred to stay in Wales, when things returned to normal: he became a Methodist minister, she was for many years a modest and respected president of *Merched y Wawr*, Daughters of the Dawn, the Welsh patriotic women's movement. Emrys and Angharad married, of course, and remained happily together for at least a year. Several of those snide young dons resumed their careers at Oxford, where they spent the rest of their lives reminiscing about the birth of Cymru Newydd under the inspired leadership of their old friend and colleague Dr Parry-Morris. For years the surviving Invitees of Train OX1 met at Oxford station for an annual reunion.

And the Llyw himself? As is well-known he lived to an advanced old age, never losing his mental alertness or his gift for apt quotation, and dying at last in his Presidential quarters on the very day he completed the eighth and final volume of his monumental work on northern Welsh rural traditions. In Oxford his face may be seen immortalized as a drip-stop in the first quadrangle of Jesus College, showing him in druidical headgear, and said by those who knew him to be a startling likeness – 'one can almost hear him talk,' people say, sometimes with a hint of affectionate disrespect. In Wales he is commemorated chiefly by the heroic statue in Parry-Morris Square, Cardiff (popularly known as The Bronze Fogey), with its celebrated inscription *Ein Llyw Cyntaf* – Our First Leader.

EIN LLYW CYNTAF

REALIST'S EPILOGUE

Well, but as everyone really knows, it did not happen like that. Britain was never occupied by the Germans, the second world war ended in a very different way, Llywelyn Parry-Morris never existed and the Welsh people were not threatened with extermination in the mountains of Eryri.

In one way, though, the fable is still developing its own truths. After 800 years of impotence, Wales has at last gained a measure of self-government from England – a very small measure of self-government, a derisory and impertinent measure the Llyw would say, but still a foot in the door. One day, without a doubt, the little country will achieve the complete fulfilment Parry-Morris envisaged for it – free to live in its own way, by its own values, bearing no grudges and cherishing no enmities.

But it will probably happen gradually, without benefit of romance. Perhaps nowadays we need no heroes or villains to populate our histories. The Marshal Zuvotzkys and the General Morgans are already beginning to feel like figures out of a discredited past, and Heinrich Schinkel ended up, I am told, as a sweet old pensioner in a senior citizens' home in Dortmund.

I like to think, though, that even outside the realm of fantasy there will always be room for such a champion as Parry-Morris – braver than he knew himself to be, not such a fool as everyone thought, and author, after all, of the imperishable *Tales and Traditions of Eifionydd* (eight calf-bound volumes, slight foxing, £150 the set).